Sloppy Joe
For Dinner

HUGO
UYTTENHOVE
With the Thursday Afternoon Sleuths

Other books by Hugo Uyttenhove:

Grand Scale Larceny: The Heist of the Flemish Primitives (2010)
Rembrandt Redux [A Tom Arden Book] (2011)
The Da Vinci Cloth [A Tom Arden Book] (2018)
Mud Cake For Breakfast [A Carolina Arbors Murder Mystery Book] (2019)
No Tacos For Lunch [A Carolina Arbors Murder Mystery Book] (2019)
Little Ace And his Big Adventures [Children's Book] (2020)
Nefertiti's Daughter [A Tom Arden Book] (2021)

© 2020 Hugo Uyttenhove
ISBN: 9798693366114
First Edition - October 2020

Notes

This book is the third collaboration between members of the Thursday Afternoon Sleuths Book Club (T.A. Sleuths) at Carolina Arbors, a Del Webb Community in Durham, North Carolina. Having read thousands of murder mystery books combined, members undertake another effort in contributing to another book in The Carolina Arbors Murder Mystery series. Again, the story takes place in their community and provides the authenticity of the environment. They introduce characters who may or may not be witnesses to the crime at hand. Story development and sewing all the parts together are the tasks of the principal author. It is up to Detective T.A. Vinder to solve the case, assisted by Officer Ramón Acosta of the Durham Police Department. As usual, the amateur sleuths of the Thursday Afternoon Sleuths Book Club participate in resolving any unanswered questions.

The author wishes to thank the T.A. Sleuths authors who have contributed to the book and helped shape the story. A special thanks to Kristin Conrad for editing the text such that it was fit for publication in its current version.

Characters

By

Sleuth Club Authors / Chapters

(In order of appearance)

George Bender	: Hollins Williams / 4
Phinn O'Hara	: Betsy Mead / 6 & 20
Mike Kreissman	: Stephanie Quinn / 10
Joe Malinski	: Leslie Abel / 12
Charlotte Beaumont	: Carol Cutler / 15
Gino Barese (young)	: Debbie Turner / 29
Gino Barese (adult)	: Nancy Ratan / 31
Hal Freese	: Norm Goldstein /39

Chapter 1

Blood Spatters

The mirrors in the lower floor men's locker room appeared fogged up, and the humidity was palpable. George heard the sound of one of the showers running the moment he walked into the room. He'd been in there several times after Tuesday bocce ball games when he needed to freshen up before a meeting upstairs. It was now Saturday evening and just not any evening. A scrumptious dinner awaited him and the men's club members down the hall. George washed his hands and used a few paper napkins to wipe one of the mirrors. He checked his perfectly groomed white hair and adjusted his black bowtie until it was perfectly centered. The tie covered the top button of his pearl white shirt that contrasted the shiny black lapels of his tuxedo. He made a small adjustment to his glasses, pushing them slightly higher on his nose. He took a deep breath inhaling the moist air hanging in the room. It had been a great evening so far, and he wanted to get back to the Varsity Room before the next speaker started. He cocked his head, wondering why someone was taking a shower at this time in the evening with the pool closed and no activities taking place downstairs, other than the gathering. Guys didn't take long showers in here, he thought. He shrugged, stepped away from the counter, and headed for the door. Before he opened it, he stopped and listened one more time. It was odd, but he had a distinct impression that the water was hitting the floor. The intermittent interruption of the steady stream by a moving body made different sounds. He contemplated the situation: someone must have forgotten to turn off the shower. He sighed deeply, slightly annoyed, and walked back in the room to the shower area. He'd have to be careful not to get wet. After all, this tuxedo wouldn't dry in time. The first stall around the corner was open, and he quickly realized that it was the second one where the hot water ran. The curtain was closed. Recognizing the slight possibility of someone in the stall, he called out a loud *Hello*. A second call still didn't elicit a response. 'Yep," he thought, "A waste of water. When were some of the residents going to learn?" He pulled the curtain away and immediately stepped back with an instant feeling of distress. He stared at the floor, and for a moment, his mouth opened, but he remained quiet. George swallowed as if pausing to assess the situation. A man was sitting slumped in the left corner with his head hanging down. Wet grey hair was hanging over his forehead. At first, he didn't recognize the man in a soaked tuxedo. The arms were lamely resting near the torso. The feet seemed oddly propped up against the opposing wall, with the knees lifted off the floor. George noticed a small pink line running from under the man's chin upward along the neck. Staring at what he perceived to be a murdered man, he took out his handkerchief, put it over the handle, and turned off the shower, only getting a small part of his sleeve wet. George didn't notice and briefly squatted down. He recognized the man as the new member of the club. He'd already forgotten his name, but he was sure it was the one who had recently moved to the neighborhood.

George stood up, leaning against the wall dividing both stalls and used his handkerchief on the curtain to pull it shut. He frowned and wiped his forehead with his jacket sleeve. He glanced at the outside door that led to the outdoor pool area. To enter from that side, one needed a key card. He didn't expect anyone to come in this time of night. He turned off the lights and exited in the hallway that led to the Varsity Room. He heard laughter and cheering as he turned away in the direction of the vending machines. Before he sat down in one of the lounge chairs, he pulled out his phone. He ran his finger through his contact list until he found Vinder's name. He checked the time: 8:10 PM. The phone rang twice, and Travis said hello.

"Detective. Sorry to bother you, but I thought it was better to call you first."

"No problem, George. What's up?"

"I'm afraid we have another murder here."

"George, you'd better be joking. I have someone here who was already very upset at the other murders in our dear Carolina Arbors."

"I just found the body detective. At Piedmont Hall."

"Damn. Anyone else aware?"

"No, as I said," George continued in a loud whisper. "I just found him here downstairs in the locker room showers."

Travis paused briefly. "All right. I tell you what to do. Get two people, one to stand guard near the locker room. No one is allowed inside that room. The other person goes with you upstairs. Make sure nobody leaves the building. While you're there, tell the receptionist to lock the building. I'll be there in five. Wait for me at the main. I'll call the station on the way over."

George hung up and hurried back to the Varsity Room. The Men's Dinner Club meeting was in full swing. The members were digging into their salad, and many were already drinking their second glass of wine or beer. Marc Baylor was giving his usually hilarious talk about the benefits of living in a 55+ community by making fun of the surmised intricacies of getting old amid the community's various parking regulations. While all eyes were on the speaker, George tapped Phinn and Mike on the shoulder, putting his index finger to his lips. He remembered that Phinn had been a police officer, so he was his first choice. Both men looked startled but followed him quietly as he motioned them to step away. Most likely, they thought a prank was at hand, but George acted seriously. Back in the hallway, Mike whispered eagerly. "So, what are you up to, George?"

"Keep this to yourselves, but there has been an incident."

Phinn poked Mike in the side and smiled. "Told you! He's going to have some fun at Marc's expense."

"This is real, guys," George whispered. "The police will be here in a minute. Follow me to the locker room. The detective I called said that someone needs to make sure nobody enters that room from now on. You, Phinn, wait outside the door. Don't go in and don't let anyone else in until the detective gets here. Mike, you come with me upstairs. We need to make sure nobody leaves the building."

Phinn and Mike's faces grew grim very quickly and did as George told them.

Upstairs, George had a quick word with Paulina at the front desk, and all the doors, except for the front automatic opening doors, were locked. George knew that locking all other doors only prevented people from entering, not leaving. Although Vinder hadn't instructed him to do so, he asked

Paulina to issue a message on the P.A. system. She complied just as she saw the detective enter the building. George imagined that the club members downstairs would not be pleased to hear that there was an emergency, that nobody was to leave the building, and that everyone was requested to come to the main foyer.

Travis nodded. "Good call, George," he said and turned to Mike. "Please stay here and make sure nobody leaves. Once everyone gathers, tell them that the police will be here shortly to resolve an incident. No need to worry everyone too much."

George noticed that Travis wasn't wearing his usual grey slacks, white shirt, and blue blazer. His brown hair seemed to have grayed a little since he'd last seen him during the Taco Truck case. Tonight, Travis had come straight from home, sporting a pair of blue Dockers and a light blue T-shirt. He wore white sneakers. Together, they headed down the stairs as the club members started to come up.

"What's going on, George?" Marc asked, looking agitated and upset. "Our main course is about to be served."

"I get it," Travis answered instead, flashing his badge. "Just go upstairs, sir. I'll be there in a short while." He continued down the stairs.

Phinn stood in front of the locker room. He appeared agitated, sweating profusely and almost out of breath. Travis briefly wondered why the man was in such a state. Perhaps, the sudden responsibility had thrown him off-kilter, but at least the man had wisely figured the P.A. announcement didn't apply to him.

"You can go now, thanks," Travis said. "Just do me a favor. When the forensics show up, bring them down here."

Phinn nodded and hurried upstairs while wiping his forehead.

Travis took his phone out while using his elbow to push open the locker room and waited for a response. "Ramón, are you on your way?"

He listened and nodded. "Make sure all doors are covered. Nobody comes in or goes out. There should be at least ten police officers to cover all doors. Put a guy outside. No cars are to leave. Stay upstairs and tell everyone to wait until I get up there to talk to them. I'll do that once the forensics show up downstairs."

George took the detective directly to the shower area. The opened curtain exposed the apparent crime scene. Travis immediately squatted down. He put on a glove and pushed the chin of the man upward. George realized that the gash he'd seen earlier extended from ear to ear with a little blood remaining in the middle. Travis stood up and sighed. "Throat slashed, most likely in this room, and I see that someone tried to clean up all the blood."

George hadn't noticed the faint streaks of watered-down blood on the walls and stared at the wall next to the urinals. He observed the same type of fine pink lines. He pointed them out to the detective.

"Most likely killed here," Travis said as the door opened, and Phinn showed in men in white overalls. He beckoned the lead expert to the shower and, after a few words, headed upstairs with George in tow.

Even before he got upstairs, he heard the buzz of voices coming from the foyer. The moment he entered the area, all quieted down. A few poker players held their chips, and the people who'd been working out in the gym were drinking from their water bottles. Several others had been in the building and were anxiously awaiting a signal to return to what they were doing. Then there were the men from the dinner club.

Neglecting comments about their dinner getting cold, Travis walked over to Ramón.

"All doors secure?"

"Total lockdown. Not sure it will help."

"Procedure, just in case," Travis answered with some annoyance. He paused. "Have all the rooms checked, top to bottom, and if anyone is left, send them up here."

Ramón nodded and started talking in his walkie-talkie as he walked to the front door.

Travis gathered all the men in tuxedos. "I'm detective Vinder. I have some bad news. Someone belonging to your group has died under suspicious circumstances." He paused and waited until the initial verbal reactions calmed down. He heard a person state that they were all there, so who could be missing? Travis continued, "Please, all the people in tuxedos follow me now."

He walked into the large conference room and closed the door once everyone was in, including Phinn who'd been relieved of his brief duties. "I need you all to wait here while I deal with the other people first. I'm sorry about your meal, but the entire downstairs area is now a crime scene."

Another quick multitude of raised voices piped down right away when Travis raised his hand.

"Tell me; is everyone in your club present?"

George counted and nodded. "All, except our newest member."

"And what's his name?" Travis asked no one in particular.

Marc Baylor stepped forward. "Carlo Messina. He just moved in two weeks ago."

Chapter 2

The Men's Dinner Club

The Medical Examiner estimated Mr. Messina died around 7:30 PM. Based on that info, Travis checked each person's alibi. Many shared alibis were making it a relatively fast process. It was about half-past nine that evening when Travis finished dealing with all the people in the foyer. Once he separately cleared each person to go, he saw them walk out of the front door. Only four people who had been in the poolroom and two in the art room had their fingerprints taken after their story revealed a few trips to the locker room that evening.

Travis figured that processing thirty people in about an hour had been a record. Most had never met the victim, which was easy to believe, given that the man had just moved to Carolina Arbors. The poker players never left their table, perhaps not wanting to leave their stack of chips unattended. After the forensic team leader gave Travis his general assessment, the detective was ready to address the men in the conference room.

"Gentlemen," he started as they were all seated in the same room where in the past he'd addressed the members of the

Thursday Afternoon Sleuths Book Club. He looked around, smiling briefly. The group reminded him of a block of penguins that had arrived with full bellies from the sea at sunset, except that this particular block was hoping to get more food. He continued. "First of all, I'd like to apologize for keeping you from your dinner tonight, but I heard..."

Marc interrupted him. "Don't worry, detective. I think we've lost our appetite, given the circumstances."

"Oh, I was just going to say that the catering staff was back downstairs, keeping your food warm."

A few men shrugged at the comment, but it remained quiet.

"Right," Travis said. "As you can imagine, we have a bit of a situation. George here told me that you guys started your monthly meeting around 7:00 PM. That puts you all in the vicinity of the men's locker room about a half-hour later."

"So, we're all suspects?" someone asked.

"I didn't mean it that way," Travis trod lightly. "One could also say *potential witnesses*." He cleared his throat and continued. "Anyway, I want to question each of you, but before we get to that, perhaps someone can tell me a little more about Mr. Messina?"

"Oh, that's easy," Marc answered. "My name is Marc Baylor. I am the president of our club."

"And the name of your club is?" Travis interjected.

"The Men's Dinner Club. I'm the person who approved Mr. Messina's membership and informed him about our rules."

"And what are some of those rules," Travis asked.

"Well, all meetings are formal with mandatory attendance. We need a full quorum of sixteen people. No exceptions."

"So, I gather you were down to fifteen a few weeks ago."

"Indeed. One of our founding members resigned because he could no longer attend to his duties as a club member. So, we added a new member rather quickly, and here we are. Unfortunately," he sighed and showed his empty hands, "We're down to fifteen again."

"You said *duties*," Travis said. "What do you mean? Treasurer, vice president, keeper of the rules, positions like that?"

"Oh, not only that! We're very active in our community and beyond. Each member brings something unique to the table, so to speak."

"Like what?"

"Well, take George, for instance. I gather you know him. He's more than a member of a book club, a guy who works out every morning, and someone who likes to travel. Like most of us, he had a job before retiring. George was a librarian, a teacher, and a few years before he retired, a vice-principal," Marc answered and glanced briefly in George's direction. "So, you might ask," he continued, returning his gaze to Travis, "How does that fit in here? Well, George is doing an incredible job in supporting some of our local middle schools. If it weren't for him, students wouldn't read a book other than their normal school books. Isn't that right, George?"

George nodded, getting slightly red in the face.

"I get the picture," Travis said. "Tell me a bit more about your rules."

"Well, we function in groups of four men. We call them quartets. Within each quartet, we function as a homogenous group of people committed to each other. These four share their history, care for each other, and are there for each other every day. It's a support group that lives underneath the currents of our everyday life. We have four such quartets. We intend to enlarge our group over the coming years to sixteen, eventually perhaps to sixty-four quartets. Sort of leaving no man in our community behind; caring for each other, regardless of religion, politics, economic status, etc. We stick up for one another and hold no secrets."

Travis took all of that in, wondering why he hadn't heard of this club before. After all, he'd lived in Carolina Arbors for several years and was familiar with most clubs. He looked at the men around the large conference table and recognized a few. He realized that these were just men doing good deeds, keeping quiet about it, and helping each other and people in the community. There seemed nothing wrong with that. The idea of a quartet sounded intriguing, and although he felt tempted to focus immediately on the other people of the foursome the victim belonged to, he waited. He pursed his lips and scratched his forehead. "Well, that's admirable. I had no idea. However, I would like to get back to my question about Mr. Messina. I asked what you could tell me about him."

"I'm sorry, detective. I was under the impression you wanted to know more about our club."

"I did, and it's interesting, indeed, because I understand the context now. What can you tell me about the victim?"

"I received a nomination in our club box about ten days ago. Any member can nominate a person who lives here."

"I see. Is it someone from your club, in other words, a person here, who nominated him?" Travis said, looking around the table. No one spoke but Marc.

"It was anonymous, and I assume it was indeed one of us."

"You can understand that, given the circumstance, I do need to ask the question: who among you nominated him?"

Nobody answered.

"I find it hard to believe it would've been an outsider who put in his name because none of you are fessing up. You would not be a suspect if you did. I just would like to know," Travis tried to reassure his audience.

Nobody moved.

"You mean to tell me that it was an outsider after all? How would that person know your protocol?"

"Oh, it may have been a past member," Marc said. "In any case, since it can be anonymous, the rules state that the nominator doesn't have to come forward."

"So, on what basis did you accept Mr. Messina into your select group?"

"There are various considerations, like his previous job and where he worked. We tend to match people in a quartet, based on original geographical locations. In this case, Carlo was from New Jersey and had done work in social services in New York."

"Do you check these things, or do you accept anything presented as fact."

"We trust our members and ex-members, so, yes to both. So far, we've had no reason to believe we shouldn't include someone."

"Thanks," Travis said. "Now, back to the events of this evening."

"Oh, no problem," Marc said, relaxing back in the chair.

Travis took his time to look at the few notes he'd made. He wondered why none of the remaining members of a quartet didn't speak up for their deceased group member. He stood up and walked toward the big window facing the foyer. He spotted only two police officers and figured the forensics team had left. It appeared that the coroner had gone because Ramón was standing near the fireplace, finishing a phone conversation.

Ramón looked up, their eyes met, and with a small jerk of his head, Travis motioned him to come over. Outside the room, he instructed Ramón to head to the victim's house and find out as much as possible. If Mr. Messina's wife were home, he'd have to give her the sad news. In any case, Ramón was to stay until Travis got there later. The detective closed the door and turned around. All eyes were still on him.

"Right," he said. "Where were we? Ah, yes, the events tonight. So, what time did Mr. Messina show up at your meeting?"

"He was early," Marc answered. "I got here around six o'clock to help with the catering service. He walked into the Varsity Room at least fifteen minutes before we started."

Travis took note. "Did anyone come here with him?"

Everyone shook his head, but it was Marc again who answered. "He came alone, I believe."

"Was he going to introduce himself tonight?"

"It was up to him, and I expected him to do so unless one of his quartet's members introduced him."

Travis kept seeing many heads nodding every time Marc spoke. Perhaps a different approach would encourage some other men to say a few words. He preferred people speaking up while in a safe and familiar group. Talking to people face to face was different because often they were more defensive, perhaps protecting vulnerabilities. Of course, he was going to speak to all of them individually. Nevertheless, for now, he wished for at least one person to speak up. He decided it was time to target a few members. "I see," he concluded. "Who among you was in the same group as Mr. Messina?"

Three men raised their hand, but it was slow and indicative of some apprehension. He recognized Mike, who just waved his hand, and Phinn, the man who had guarded the locker room earlier. He looked at him directly. "How long have you known your newest member?"

Phinn took out his handkerchief and wiped his forehead. Before he could answer, a tall man raised his hand and spoke. "Tonight was our first encounter, detective. We did talk for about thirty minutes or so before he left the table. I'm not sure what we can add *here*."

Travis had a gut feeling that the man wanted to talk somewhere else, grasping the meaning of the last word in the answer. Travis figured for now that the other members didn't know the murdered man, except perhaps for the person, if present tonight, who introduced Carlo to the club. He nodded. "Why don't you three follow me? The rest of you stay here. I should be back in a short while. By the way, I just want to check. The caterer has no problem bringing up some food for you guys. Any takers?"

No one responded audibly. Travis saw Marc shaking his head.

Travis left the room with the trio in tow. He headed for the room on the other side of the foyer. Along the way, he briefly talked to one of the officers. He instructed him not to let anyone leave the meeting room except for a bathroom break, in which case another officer would have to go along.

The three men sat down on the comfortable couches in the middle of the room. Travis grabbed a chair from one of the tables and put it down, facing the men.

"Let's start with some names and some of your background, and then we can talk about Carlo." He'd taken out his notebook from his back pocket.

The tall man spoke up first. "Joe Malinski. Retired NY City detective. We're here to help you solve this crime, detective."

Travis was pleasantly surprised and glad he read the man's intentions correctly, signaling that this conversation was better to have away from the other club members. Before he could respond, the man next to him introduced himself.

"We met earlier. I'm Phinn O'Hara. I was a cop with a beat in Brooklyn for twenty years."

"And I'm Mike Kreissman," the smaller man said. "I was a cab driver in Manhattan and retired early. I moved here two years ago."

Travis wrote it all down. The New York connection was undeniable. He was interested in why the victim had become part of their quartet. "So, who left your group, and how did you get to know Mr. Messina?"

"Easy, detective," Joe answered. "You see, when Jim fell away, we had two choices: adopt a member from another quartet or accept a newly proposed member. We talked with Marc and discussed the matter among ourselves. In this case, we didn't want the other quartets to change, so we accepted Mr. Messina after he was nominated."

"Did any of you talk to him?"

"I did," Joe volunteered. "I met him about a week ago. I know I led you to believe in there that it was the first time I'd seen him, but let me explain."

"I'm listening," Travis said, sitting back, uncrossing his legs.

"As a newcomer, he didn't belong to any club yet. Marc suggested I talk to Mr. Messina, and I contacted him right away. His background seemed interesting enough, and since he was from our area, I didn't object and told him what to expect. He said he would be glad to join. I didn't mention that earlier because, as a quartet, we handle our issues and keep others out of it."

"Did you recommend him to Marc?"

"No, we don't know who did," Phinn answered. "I suspect Jim did since he lives only a few houses down from Messina's house, but I didn't ask."

"What's Jim's last name?"

"Whitman. He's not doing too well, by the way. One of the reasons he left. He's also a founder of our club."

"I see," Travis said, trying to figure out how it was that they had each other's back, yet let a member just peel off because he wasn't doing well. He continued, "Had any of you met Mr. Messina before tonight?"

Both Mike and Phinn shook their heads.

"We were going to sit together and sort some things out," Joe offered. "We don't grill a new member. We see what comes up in a conversation and let it lead us. Once we find common ground, we make that the issue of the day. Regardless of that, we have each other's back, as Marc explained."

Travis reflected on that for a second. How did this 'having your back' go? Could members resign? Something to follow up on later, perhaps. "So, you guys didn't know him before he moved here." It wasn't a question really, and Travis didn't expect an answer. Mike appeared to want to elaborate a bit, and that's what Travis had hoped he would do.

"You know, detective, as a cabbie, you meet a lot of people. So, who knows? Did I ever take him for a ride? I wouldn't know. You also got the fact that after a while, a lot of people look alike in your rearview mirror, you see. It kind of all blends together, you see. I mean, I can tell a broad from a young punk, of course, but all blondes start to look alike after a while if you get my drift?"

Travis sat up but didn't take notes. Mike was a talker, and he planned on interviewing him later in detail. Joe seemed a good guy but a little vague as if not comfortable with his current situation. Phinn, on the other hand, appeared a little gloomy. Travis realized that if you walked the beat for such a long time, you'd seen it all. That sort of person becomes hardened by the visual elements of crime, much like criminals themselves did, but differently. Most likely, he'd grown discouraged over time, realizing that nothing would ever change. Travis was interested in all three men and made a decision. "Why don't the three of you stay here for a while? I'll go and talk to the others, and I'll be back in a while. If you need a break, talk to one of the officers in the foyer. They're staying here all evening."

The men nodded, seemingly not very clear why Travis wanted to keep them separate from the others. Travis was sure they'd figure it out soon. He needed them to talk with each other. Perhaps sort some things out because if there were anything amiss regarding their short relationship with the victim, the ex-detective would find out.

Travis returned to the conference room and called each remaining member separately to the area near the back windows in the foyer. He wrote down their names in groups determined by their quartet. All in all, they were a decent group of men who seemed more shocked than elusive when he talked with them in the meeting room. None of them knew Mr. Messina from before and hadn't seen him before the dinner meeting. He finished around 10:30 PM. Piedmont Hall should have been closed earlier, but since it was a crime scene, it would only close when Travis decided to do so.

During his brief questionings of the men, he once and a while glanced at the other room where the three men sat, clearly visible through the large windows. There never seemed to be a lot of conversation going on. The fireplace partly obscured Joe. Perhaps he was doing the talking. As soon as Travis finished with the last man, he closed his notebook and walked downstairs. The section to his right leading from the locker room to the yoga room, which he knew was also called the Cardinal Room, was closed off with yellow tape. Forensics had built in the possibility that they might have to return. He walked over to the last room on his left, known as the Southport Room, where the caterers had cleaned up everything. From his earlier quick encounter, he'd learned that they were neighbors, husband and wife, who were helping out the catering service as a favor. All the food had cooled and been stowed away. The husband and wife were sitting on coolers, waiting for him.

"Sorry about all that," Travis said. "I guess you guys can leave. Perhaps you can return the food or donate it?"

"We've arranged for delivery to a food kitchen in the morning," the man said.

The two each picked up a cooler and headed for the door. Travis realized that although he questioned them earlier, he wanted to make sure he hadn't overlooked anything. "Hold on just a sec," he said. "I need to ask you something."

The heavy coolers hit the floor again.

"Did anyone else enter this room between six and eight tonight?"

"No, we were the only ones setting the tables while keeping the food hot," the woman answered. "We then served the salad."

"During that time, did either of you go back out to your car?"

"We were here the whole time," the man replied, getting ready to pick up a cooler again. "We had everything we needed."

"Wait," the woman said. "Remember Paulo?" She looked at her husband and then turned to Travis. "They'd forgotten to include the serving utensils at the restaurant, and he brought them over just about seven. He stayed for a short while and then left, heading for the hallway. I assume he went back to the restaurant."

"Fair enough," Travis said. "You guys can go. I have your info."

They nodded, and as soon as they put the coolers on a small cart, they headed for the elevator. Travis reminded himself to pick up the door movement report from the front desk later. If any other door than the main entrance had been opened with a key card or propped open for a while, it would surely show. He walked back upstairs, ready to spend more time questioning the trio before heading out to Mr. Messina's home.

Chapter 3

Maureen's Take

It was a bit before midnight when Travis tiptoed into the bedroom. The TV was on, and Maureen sat up when she heard him turn on the faucet in the bathroom.

"You were gone quite a while. What happened?"

Travis walked back into the bedroom and sat down on his side of the bed. "Unfortunately, another case. Not sure what to make of it yet," he said and yawned.

"Not at Carolina Arbors..." She turned off the TV.

"Afraid so," he said. "Also, not sure it has anything to do with this place, but I spent some time with three neighbors who haven't told me everything yet."

Maureen was fully awake. "Why is this happening here? I knew Durham had its share of crime when we moved, but nothing ever happened here at the Arbors until last year, Travis."

"I can't answer that," he said, reaching over and patting her leg, leaving his hand resting there. "We've discussed this before, but every community has its problems. Some are inherent, and some are incidental. I think we're dealing with the latter. Just bad luck, I guess."

"Yeah, well, I don't like it. I wish you'd do your job a little further away from home. Tell me, what happened?"

Travis told her the story in general lines, including the fact that just before he came home, he had a strange conversation with the three men of the quartet. He was sure they still had not told him everything, and he suspected one of them might even have been lying. For a moment, he contemplated that perhaps all three were not telling the whole truth, because they had 'each other's back.' They were the first on his list tomorrow. "Then again," he paused, taking off his T-shirt. "I don't see why the one guy who's an ex-detective would lie."

"What about the dead man?"

"Ah, yes. That man moved here alone. Ramón was at the house when I got there and had written up a report. He'd found the house unlocked. The kitchen was in use, but the refrigerator had but a few basic things in it. The master bedroom looked slept in, and that was about it. There was one single pillow on the bed and man's clothing only in the small walk-in closet. All the walls were still bare, and there were at least fifteen unopened boxes in the garage. We'll go through all that tomorrow. Ramón said he was glad he didn't have to give anyone the bad news."

"You said something about a men's club. What did you call it again?"

"The Men's Dinner Club."

"So, all they do is eat dinner together? Why didn't they go somewhere else for dinner?"

"Good question. I'll ask the club's talkative president," Travis said while getting up.

"And who's ever heard of a group of men splitting into quartets. What are they? A golf group, a music group? It seems silly to me."

"Again, dear, I'm going to find out. One thing for sure is that the members treat all of the intricacies of their club very seriously."

"Including their selection committee?"

"I believe there isn't one."

"I'd rather think that any club with lofty ambitions would recruit diligently and vet people applying for membership. Are you saying anyone can join?"

"Only if recommended by a member or ex-member."

"Who recommended your victim?"

"He's not my victim, Maureen," Travis said from the bathroom where he was about to brush his teeth.

"But who did?"

"I don't know."

Water was running, and Maureen held off her questions until Travis came to bed.

"You know that this is the clue to everything, right?"

"What is?"

"The person who recommended him."

"It was anonymous."

"There's no such thing. Who runs that club anyway?"

"A Marc Baylor. I've met him a few times at the wine club when we used to go."

"I signed us up for the next meeting, by the way."

"Ah, good. I hope I can make it."

"That would be nice. A few nights at home without a case."

"Well, crime doesn't take a vacation, and..."

"I know, I know," Maureen interrupted. "I tell you, find out who wanted the dead guy in the club, find out why and you'll have your motive and the murderer. Sleep tight." She fluffed up her pillow and tucked in for the night.

"Good night, dear," Travis said. He stayed awake for quite a while, knowing that Maureen had nailed all the points he already identified. He had no answers for now.

Chapter 4

George Reflects

George opened the door of his home at 11:00 PM to be greeted with a kiss from his golden retriever Chip and a concerned look from his wife Betsy. He'd called her several hours earlier about the murder at Piedmont Hall. She already knew that he was the one who discovered the body. She gave him a quick hug.

"So, what's the latest update on this killing? Has Vinder found the culprit yet?"

George said, "The police are still at the clubhouse."

"Had you met Carlo? I don't recall you mentioning him before."

"Tonight was the first time. Seeing him dead in the shower was the closest I'd been to the man tonight. You remember that I was at my mother's side when she died from her heart attack and saw my father shortly after he died from cancer, but I've never seen a murdered person before. His throat was slashed," George said, almost matter-of-factly. He pushed his glasses higher on his nose and loosened his bowtie.

"Oh, dear, how terrible! I can't imagine how you must feel. Sit down and relax. Can I get you anything?"

"No, thanks. Not in the mood for eating, and I had some wine earlier. At my age, a little goes a long way."

"This is the third murder we have had in the Arbors in a year. The villages in Midsomer Murders are starting to look safer! What's going on in our community?"

"I wish I could tell you. I was hoping Marc or the other members of the quartet Carlo belonged to can help out the detective, but it appears that no one knew him very well. Marc said Carlo was nominated anonymously, and no one admitted to nominating him or had any idea of who might have done so."

Betsy asked, "What about Jim? He just left the club. Maybe he nominated him to take his place."

"Possibly, but Jim is having a lot of health issues at the moment. I have not seen him since his stroke about a month ago. I assume Vinder will talk to him tomorrow."

"Good. Are you sure I can't get you anything?"

"Honestly, I'm tired and just want to chat a few minutes before going to bed. It's been quite the night."

"I understand, dear. Tell me, what else did Marc say about the man?"

"He said that Carlo was from New Jersey and worked in social services. His location fit in well with the others in the group since they're all from the New York City area."

"So, who were the others in his quartet?"

"There's Phinn O'Hara, a former Brooklyn policeman. You probably remember him from the Wine Club meeting where he told everyone about his exploits dealing with the mafia in the Big Apple. It reminded me of the Godfather movies. Then there's Mike Kreissman. He used to be a taxi driver in Manhattan. Our neighbor, Joe Malinski, is the third guy. We all know he and his wife moved here after retiring from his job as a New York City detective. Those three are very close and had a lot in common. I was wondering if any of them had ever met Carlo."

"Do you think one of them might have known Carlo from before?"

"I have no clue. With Carlo, they had a group all from the New York area. Phinn and Joe have told me several stories about their exploits in New York with mob killings and shoot-outs. Mike just knew all the places they mentioned. I'm not sure what Carlo's story was. Perhaps he worked in the City."

Betsy asked, "What about the man's wife and family? They must be devastated."

George responded, "They must be. I'm sure the police went to the house tonight."

"Well, it is so sad – dying alone. I hope the investigators find the killer quickly. Could someone from outside the community have killed him?"

"It would've been difficult. You can't get into the shower area from the back entrance without a key card, and there were too many people in the Varsity Room area for someone to be unnoticed using the staircase. Not only are key card entries registered automatically, but there are several cameras. I'm surprised that whoever did it was able to get away with it. There couldn't have been much time to murder Carlo and leave without worrying about someone coming to use the bathroom."

"Are you going to call a meeting of your Mystery Book Club and get everyone involved again? I joke, but this is rather serious. I never envisioned living in a criminal neighborhood, especially a 55+ community on Durham's outskirts."

"Let's not exaggerate, dear. The first murder was truly a revenge killing that only happened because the parties ended up living in our community. The second murder had nothing to do with us because the victim and the murderer were outside people. Of course, we don't know anything about motive or a connection with us in this case," George sighed. "Nevertheless, yes, I'll send everyone in our book club a message tomorrow. Who knows, maybe someone knows something about Carlo or saw something strange in our neighborhood tonight. Right now, I need to try to get some sleep.

Chapter 5

Checking The Timeline

The back of the clubhouse still had yellow tape up, identifying a crime scene area. The tape stretched between the pillars and the door handles of the entrances next to the men's locker room door. It was just about eight-thirty Sunday morning. Travis pensively stared at the brown door to the locker room. It had bothered him all night that the lockdown the previous evening had seemed perfect. Granted that nobody could come into the building except through the front entrance where police officers had been, it was entirely possible to leave the building through any other door that wasn't covered. Yet, nobody had entered or left except for himself, officers, and the people he had questioned. All entry spots were electronically monitored. If someone used a card at any door, there'd be a timestamp and an I.D. of the person using the card registered on the security computer. That only worked for people entering, of course. Only four cameras recorded when there was movement in certain areas in the building and outside, but they'd seen nothing suspicious on the outside near the downstairs men's locker room.

The last time someone had entered the room from that spot yesterday was at 5:30 PM. An elderly neighbor, who, judging by swimming trunks and a towel draped over his shoulder, may have come from the pool and entered the locker room. His baseball cap was a little skewed as if he'd just remembered it before he left and had thrown it on his head, not bothering to straighten it out. For obvious reasons, there were no cameras in the room. Unfortunately, inside the building, there were no cameras in the downstairs area. So, it couldn't be determined when that man had left the room. Forensics had lifted a multitude of fingerprints from doors and handles. Trying to compare them to the prints of people who visited the clubhouse by going house to house in the neighborhood to find a match was a waste of time. Last night, Ramón had double-checked and determined that the door hadn't been opened again after 5:30 PM and that all other downstairs doors remained shut until the police had shown up. The recording of the two upstairs cameras had shown residents coming and leaving through the main entrance and the back door. Possibly, the killer hadn't left the building, which meant that he must have been inside when he ordered the lockdown.

The coroner already confirmed that Carlo died from bleeding out after the slashing of his throat. There was no evidence of a fierce struggle. The murderer must have been waiting and surprised the victim in front of the urinals. From the evidence on the walls, the murder had taken place near the left urinal opposite the showers. Had someone entered or left that room between Carlo's and George's entrances. George? Yes, he had found the body. Could he be? No way. George's clothes were clean. Where did that thought originate? Travis shook his head and walked away from the back. As mysteries go, this one would take some work to solve. He walked around the building and entered through the automatic front door.

Ramón was waiting for him in the front lobby.

"Did you confirm he was single? No wife left in New Jersey?"

"Not a single sign of a woman in his life, Travis. Also, everything is in his name only."

"Have you talked to someone at the sales office?"

"I met them as they walked in at eight."

"Talk to me."

"Mr. Messina closed on the house three weeks ago and moved in sixteen days ago," Ramón said, checking his notes. "Julia is checking where he moved from and should have some more information later. I'm also going to check tomorrow morning with the closing attorney."

"Good work, Ramón. Look for a contact in New Jersey. I may need to talk to some people there."

"You think of going up there?"

"Not right away. I know a detective I worked with when I lived in Upstate New York. For now, we have other things to do here first."

"Did anyone see anything suspicious last night? I heard you talked to about forty people."

"If anyone did, they didn't tell me. A few men haven't told me everything, so I'm not sure whether these are witnesses or, who knows, are somehow involved."

"How many are you talking about?"

"Just three for now."

"Will you have them go to the station?"

"They'll be in by ten. First, I want to take another look at the recordings and the entry log. Just in case I missed something."

"Can I join?"

Travis walked to the front desk and motioned Ramón to come along.

Melanie had the morning shift at the front desk. She took Travis and Ramón to the office where, together with Almira in the back office, they selected the stored videos on the security computer. There wasn't anything more to report from the outside camera other than the swimmer. The front door camera showed residents coming and going with several men in tuxedos hurrying downstairs. The catering couple had come in through the side entrance using their key card, and Travis got the confirmation that one of the restaurant employees had come in with the serving spoons. He also left about five minutes later.

What interested him the most were movements starting at 7:30 PM? Nothing unusual showed up until Almira made a silent comment, softly saying a person's name. Ramón was yawning and went in search of coffee. Travis had just looked at the clock on the wall, keeping in mind that he had to get to the station to talk to the trio of men. When he heard Almira faintly say the name *Whitman* while she saw an older man in a bathing suit, wearing the goofy cap and a towel flung over his shoulder, he said, "Pause that!" He looked at the time on the screen, and it was 7:39 PM.

"That's the same guy we saw at 5:30, isn't it?" he asked no one in particular.

"Yes, that's Mr. Whitman," Melanie confirmed.

"But he supposedly isn't doing very well. What was he doing here? He'd recently resigned from that men's club, yet he's around for about two hours?"

There wasn't any response. Ramón returned with two cups of coffee and saw Travis's puzzled look. "Everything okay?"

"Why would someone who went swimming, go to the locker room to make his way upstairs, and wait to leave two hours later?"

Melanie offered a possibility with a smile: "He probably went to the gym and may have spent some time in the hot tub. He was always fond of that, and I seem to recall he used to do that often. Honestly, though, I haven't seen him in weeks. "

"I'm surprised that he's so active. What I understood from the club members yesterday was that he had a stroke. Are you sure it's Mr. Whitman?"

"Yes! He's got his trademark pink towel and pink flip flops."

"I see. Can you get Mr. Whitman's address for me?"

"Sure," Almira responded and went over to a large cabinet.

"That's odd," Ramón agreed. "If he's active, why isn't he a member still?"

"It isn't only that," Travis said, getting up and grabbing his jacket. "He's the one who was replaced by Mr. Messina in his quartet. What would be the chance that he's also the one who suggested the murder victim as a member? Let's go and find out."

Melanie handed Travis a post-it-note on which she'd written the address.

Tuttle Road was only five minutes away. Checking the address briefly, they walked over to the house and rang the doorbell. A frail woman with snow-white hair opened the door.

"Can I help you," she said, her voice firm, belying her appearance.

"Detective Vinder and Officer Acosta from the Durham Police, ma'am."

"Oh, what's wrong?"

"There was an incident at the clubhouse last night, and we were wondering if your husband was there last night."

"Jimmy? Oh, no, detective, he's been in bed for almost two months since his stroke. You see, he can barely walk. So, no, he wasn't there last night. I'm sure he wished he could go out, but I'm sorry to say he wasn't there."

Travis slowly stroked the stubbles on his chin and looked at Ramón, who stared back at him with raised eyebrows.

"I'm confused. We have a timestamp of Mr. Whitman's entrance through one of the lower back doors where he swiped his key card to enter the building."

"Well, I don't understand either, detective."

"Is his card in the house? Ramón asked.

"Come in," the woman said. "I'll go find it. Just a minute."

Travis and Ramón stepped inside, and they heard the woman ask her husband where his card was. He answered something they couldn't understand. Travis took a picture frame from a counter. It appeared to be a picture of the Whitmans only a few years ago. Mr. Whitman did resemble the older man on the security video. He heard a few more exchanges behind a now closed bedroom door, and soon the woman appeared again.

"He says he lost it weeks ago."

"Oh," Travis said, immediately thinking of all sorts of possibilities why that card went missing. "I agree it couldn't have been your husband at Piedmont Hall last night. Sorry to have troubled you. I hope he gets better."

"I hope so too. Glad to have been of help, detective."

Ramón stopped in the driveway. "What do you think is going on here?"

"Not sure," Travis said. "We have him on camera, yet, I have to believe his wife. If he can't walk, we may have an imposter, or, if he can walk, he's been lying to his wife, and he got out for a few hours. That would make him a suspect."

"Why don't we check his medical records?"

"I don't have a reason not to believe her, Ramón."

"So, an imposter it is?"

"We need to take another look at that video. Get a copy of that and bring it to the station. I need to go soon because the first of those guys will be waiting."

"On it!" Ramón said as they walked back to their cars. "I'm also following up with George Bender, as we discussed last night."

Chapter 6

Phinn O'Hara

It was ten after nine, and the parking lot at the Durham Police Station was nearly empty. Phinn O'Hara decided to wait in his car since he was twenty minutes early for his appointment with the detective. In his mind, he'd prepared for the conversation all morning after a restless night. His emotions had gotten the better of him since standing guard at that door. He drank three cups of coffee this morning and realized he should have stuck to one because now he had a tough time calming down. He wanted to stay focused if he was to give an impassive statement this morning. He'd called Mike and Joe earlier to see whether they wanted to drive together, but they declined given that each had a different appointment time with the detective. During the short conversations the evening before, they each confirmed that they didn't know Carlo and that they'd welcome helping in the investigation.

Sitting in the car, staring at the remainder of the coffee in his cup, Phinn thought about the events last night. He figured that George had picked him to guard the door to the downstairs locker room because he'd been in law enforcement. Regardless, waiting at the locker room door by himself and seeing everyone head upstairs after hearing the announcement of the building's lockdown instilled in him some sense of importance in having taken up this guarding position. It bothered him a bit that George hadn't shared the nature of the *incident* that caused all the commotion. Once he felt sure about being the only one downstairs, all that was left was to wait for the police to show up. Phinn soon had gotten edgy. Feeling that sudden tenseness, he wished he had a cigarette. He rejected that almost immediately because the need to find out what happened behind that locker room door rapidly became more powerful. He hadn't heard any sirens, and besides a slight buzz of all the voices upstairs, everything remained quiet. Right then, he made a decision. Using his back, he pushed open the door and briskly walked in the room, looking left and right. When he got to the back door, he hadn't noticed anything. *"An incident? What was George talking about?"*

He deeply inhaled the moist air in the room and turned around. To his right, he noticed the showers. The first shower curtain was open. He stepped in the area quickly and, with his left forearm, pushed aside the other closed shower curtain. The gruesome scene staring at him brought an immediate rush of anguish.

"Not murder! Not here!" Hadn't he seen enough crime as a New York City cop?" Phinn ranted silently to himself. He felt bile rise in his throat as he looked down at the body. He fought to stave off the once-familiar panic mode that tightened his chest. Here he was alone, staring down at a twisted body propped up against the shower wall. The new guy in their quartet no less! Phinn's naturally wavy red hair lay sweat-soaked

and plastered against his skull, and the freckles on his face looked pale against his already blanched damp skin. His breath came in shallow pants as his stomach lurched around the just consumed salad. Observing the scene, he began wondering if the killer was trying to make a statement, or is this simply the way the body landed. *"Wait, no..."* he thought. *"This isn't my investigation, not my business. Stay clear of this one."*

Now Phinn wished he hadn't gone to the Men's Dinner Club. His wife, Mary, was at home, reading. It seemed since they retired, she always read books. She loved her book club and her silly murder mystery books. He wasn't happy sitting around since he left the force. It made him edgy and nervous.

He remembered saying *"Damn"* out loud in that locker room as a shiver crawled up his spine, and his stomach flipped over into a sour knot. The creepy crawly feel of adrenaline had moved up his body like slow electric quivers. It even settled in his jaw as he clenched, looking at the dead body of their newest club member. He ran his fingers through his damp hair and walked back to his assigned spot outside, trying to catch his breath. That's when he heard people coming down the stairs. He had recognized George's voice and wiped his forehead with his right sleeve. He pulled at the bottom of his jacket and brushed off some imagined spots. He figured he'd been in the room at most a minute, convinced he hadn't touched anything. That was last night.

Checking the clock in his car, he realized he should be getting inside. He didn't want to disappoint the detective.

About five minutes later, Travis collected Phinn from the waiting room. He didn't want to use an interrogation room for several reasons, so he showed Phinn into a small conference room with more comfortable chairs.

"Thanks for coming in today, Mr. O'Hara," Travis started. "A cup of coffee?"

"Sure, I can do with another one," Phinn smiled nervously, figuring he'd be polite.

Travis poured two cups from the pot. "Black?"

"Just some sugar, thanks," Phinn answered.

Sitting down again, Travis got out his notepad and took a sip of the hot coffee. "Tell me a little about yourself," he started. "When did you move to the Arbors?"

Phinn relaxed a bit. At least the detective hadn't started with the event from last night. "We moved from Brooklyn and came here to retire and relax. I love doing fun things, like playing all kinds of games, card games, riddles, and competitive games. My wife, Mary, encouraged me to socialize, so I made it a point to engage with others in this community. Besides the men's club, I joined a poker and pickleball club. Oh, and I just joined the bocce ball club."

"Good for you," Travis smiled, looking up from a still blank page. "I once heard someone say that this is like Disneyland for adults. It must be quite a change from your work in New York, right?"

"You can say that again! I never had time for anything. But here, it's different, you know. Just last week, I went with a group of friends to an escape room. That was a blast! I had no idea what an escape room was. Apparently, they pop up all over the country. We spent an hour in a make-believe room, and there was a scenario with all sorts of perplexing puzzles to identify and solve as a team. But don't misunderstand me: I also like to be at home with Mary, something that had been missing when I was a cop in tough Brooklyn neighborhoods I used to patrol."

"I get that. I'm still in that boat," Travis agreed. "Take last night, for instance. I didn't get home till after eleven. And that's the case several nights a week, and depending on some cases, during the weekend."

"Yeah, I know. It didn't make it any easier that for years I battled the criminal infiltration of organized crime on my beat."

"Really? How did you cope with that?"

Phinn immediately thought about his life-changing traumatic experience, which had left him with feelings of doubt and inadequacy. How much should he share with Detective Vinder? He sat up in the chair and drank some coffee, organizing his thoughts. He'd been a good cop, tough but honest. No reason not to share some things with the detective, he figured. "I got very close to nailing some big boys, but they beat me to it. Literally. Years ago, I was abducted outside of my home and brutally beaten at a warehouse owned by one of the crime families. I was hit from behind and didn't remember much after I regained consciousness. My hands still tied behind my back. Although a SWAT team stormed in a few minutes later, the damage was already done. I remember a nauseating feeling of terror. At the hospital, they told me I had two broken ribs and traumatic brain injury. They cut off part of my right index finger as if those goons wanted to make sure I'd never fire a gun again. Little did they know I am left-handed," he chuckled.

"Wow, that's quite a story, Phinn," Travis said, unsure what to ask him next. He shook his head in disbelief. "You've been through some hard times."

Phinn nodded. He didn't bother mentioning his later diagnosis of PTSD and that bits and pieces of his memory had gradually returned over the years. "Yeah, I did. I had good friends, though, including my cousin Patrick. He's a medical examiner in the City. He's the one that referred me to a brain treatment center."

"Did you recover to go back to your beat?"

"Nope, I didn't. At least that's what my superiors believed. They put me on desk duty, using my partially missing digit as an excuse to keep me off the streets. Eventually, my lack of ability to concentrate effectively ended my career after twenty-five years on the force. I did get a job for many years as a safety firearms instructor and trained security people the following years."

"I'm glad that worked out for you somehow," Travis concluded after taking a few notes. He felt he had enough background on Phinn for now and wanted to talk with him about the current case.

"I appreciate your coming in today because I do want to talk a bit about last night."

Phinn shifted in his seat and drank from his cup. 'Uh-huh," is all he could muster.

"I think I asked you last night, but just to complete my notes, did anyone enter or exit the locker room while you were standing guard there?"

"Not while I was there," Phinn confirmed.

"And you didn't leave your spot?"

The hesitation was apparent. Phinn was considering the repercussion of lying and not lying about his brief observation of the crime scene. He noticed that Vinder was raising his eyebrows and made a decision. Either answer didn't matter in the investigation, he thought. "Not that I recall." He shook his head.

"I see," Travis said, jotting down something. "Now, it appears that Mr. Messina had just become a member of the club and your quartet. Did you meet with him before last night?"

"I didn't. I did talk with the man briefly last evening as our dinner meeting was getting started. We quickly established some rapport since we were from the New York City area. I didn't have time to ask what his career was before moving here because Mike and Joe showed up and started talking to him. I went over to the bar to get a glass of wine."

"Do you know who might have suggested him as a member?"

"No idea. As Marc told you, nominations are by a member or ex-member, and we accept that until we get a feel for the person." Travis had been waiting for the *'having each other's back'* speech again. "So, what if that person doesn't work out in your quartet?"

"That's why we have the first month of trial membership. We get to know the new person during a dinner gathering and when we work on some project or help each other out with mundane tasks."

"So he was, so to speak, on probation," Travis concluded.

"Yes, you could say it that way."

"Quite some initial outlay for a tuxedo without a guarantee of making it as an accepted member."

"Maybe so, detective. As long as I have been in the club, every new member remains after their trial period."

"I see," Travis said, completing a few more notes. The club seemed to have odd rules which appeared a bit lax. There was a knock on the door, and Ramón stuck his head in the room.

"Mind if I join you?" he said.

"No problem," Travis said. "We're about to wrap things up here."

"It's just that I briefly talked with George as a follow up to last night's conversation. He'd been thinking about something last night that bothered him, and perhaps Mr. O'Hara can help us solve a strange situation."

"Perhaps. What's Mr. Benders' cryptic problem?" Travis asked.

"Simple. George remembers closing the curtain of the shower stall with the body. Yet, when he went back inside with you, the curtain was pulled back. He was concerned about why that was the case."

Travis looked at Phinn. It was a concerned look, and Phinn caught that immediately. He couldn't bear to be a suspect. His nerves began to tingle as his cortisol shot up. This interview wasn't over yet.

"Yes, Mr. O'Hara," Travis started. "You realize that something is odd here. You told me that no-one entered the room, yet, someone moved the curtain while you were standing guard."

Phinn felt that same panic attack coming on. Why did he lie anyway? He'd totally forgotten about the curtain. He'd have to confess now, and the detective would never forget that he lied. He briefly pondered how to answer this and sat back, trying to appear calm. "Well, George came to fetch me to stand guard. Someone could've entered after he left and before I got there. Anything's possible, right?"

"How much time do you think passed between George leaving and you coming down?"

"Two to three minutes, I guess."

"And being a policeman yourself, you didn't want to check things out?"

"Oh, I wanted to all right," Phinn admitted.

"I would venture to say, Mr. O'Hara, that anyone entering that room, finding the body and moving the curtain would have done one of two things," Ramón said. "Either one would run like hell and alert someone about the discovery, or one already knew would want a closer look, without telling someone." Travis paused. "Which person do you think it is?"

Phinn recognized the trap. In the first case, he and George would have run into this person. If it was the second case, he was the person in question. He cleared his throat and spoke quietly. "I told you that no person entered while I was standing there. I, on the other hand, did leave briefly to check inside. Technically I wasn't standing guard anymore, so I didn't completely lie, detective."

"You're a cop, dammit," Travis shot back. "You moved that curtain. You went against my instructions, and you violated a crime scene!"

Phinn remained quiet, averting his eyes from the two men in front of him. He realized the stupidity of not having come clean last night or a while ago. He imagined his hands tied behind his back again. It was as if some bully from the Fortimare Family was yelling at him. His head started hurting. He felt his heart pulse in his chest. His face suddenly felt flushed, and he noticed that he was becoming light-headed. Even his breathing was labored. He tried to say something meaningful to the detective, but his eyes turned upward as he fainted and crashed to his side, where Ramón was just able to catch him before his head hit the floor.

Chapter 7

George's Take

Phinn O'Hara had regained consciousness on the small couch in the conference room. A paramedic who happened to be on the premises was tending to him and stayed until he felt comfortable that the man could drive back home.   Travis had said that he had no further questions and had gone to his office with Ramón.

The officer pulled out his small notebook and sat down across from the desk. "So, yes, Mr. Bender had a lot to share this morning. He seemed to recall more details as he calmed down after the adrenaline rush he must have experienced. Finding a murdered man in that condition must have been unsettling."

"I agree. Given time, several people will start remembering things from last night. Some things may be a little distorted or useless, but there may be enough to go on because we're nowhere regarding a motive or suspect."

"In that respect, Mr. Bender, for one, is doing much better. For about an hour, he and I discussed the things that happened last evening, and you already know what he recalled about that curtain."

"That was timely," Travis agreed. "I still wonder why Mr. O'Hara lied about going in there at first. I hate it when people use semantics to evade telling the truth and think they can get away with it. I have a feeling we haven't heard the last of him. Frankly, I'm sure I haven't finished with him. Anyway, what else did George remember?"

"We talked quite a bit about the men's club. He told me that you already know most of what he was telling me. What impressed me most was the inherent buddy system in their club. I got the feeling that a lot of the men here need some form of a support system. George told me that many used to run a business or were managers working with others in teams. A few years after they retire, they often realize that they're missing the interaction with others. They don't need to make big decisions anymore and are not happy sitting around doing nothing. They prefer working with others on a meaningful project in the community. Some organize and participate in reading programs in schools; some help out a neighbor with something that requires physical work. He told me one quartet is involved with a church in one of their mission projects, and another one is helping out with local Habitat for Humanity."

"That's quite a bit more that Marc, their president, shared last evening. What else did he say about last night?"

"George was there early as it was his job to set up the bar and coordinate the last-minute details with the caterers. There are two sets of stairs going downstairs to the Varsity Room. For the occasion, curtains were drawn in the hallway at both ends. This gives more privacy when there's an event. As members came in, they all headed for the bar, giving George a chance to say hello to most of them."

"That's good to know. With the curtains closed, it is impossible to see who uses the stairs. Did he mention with whom the murder victim came in?"

"Yes, he did. He's pretty sure he walked in by himself. At the bar, he made himself a bourbon and ginger ale. However, it's interesting to note that Joe Malinski and Mike Kreissman were standing under the large TV screen staring at him. He saw Mike nudge Joe with his elbow to draw attention to Mr. Messina at the self-service bar. They turned around and talked to each other, but George couldn't hear what they said as about ten others were talking loudly."

"Interesting. What about O'Hara?"

"He saw O'Hara walk up to Messina when he got to their assigned table. They talked for a short while, and then Malinski and Kreissman joined them. At that point, O'Hara walked away toward the bathroom."

"Did he say at what time all that transpired?"

"Well, before they sat down for their appetizers. It was around five to seven."

"And did he see O'Hara return from the bathroom area?"

"No, but when they all had sat down, their quartet was complete."

"I know it would be too good to be true, but did George happen to see the victim head for the bathroom?"

"Unfortunately, he didn't. However, when he headed for the bathroom himself, he's sure he'd seen two full tables and only one person missing from the O'Hara table."

"So, one of the three men must know when Messina left, or at least have an approximate time."

"I agree. Did you ask O'Hara?"

"No, I didn't get that far. Don't worry; I'll revisit that. I'm talking with the two others from that table this morning, and I hope we'll get a good indication of that time. Together with the estimated time of death we got from the Medical Examiner, we should be able to put some more points on the timeline."

"Do you want me to sit in on those?"

"Not really," Travis said, looking at his phone. "I need to collect Mr. Kreissman from the waiting room. Check to see if Mr. O'Hara is still around. If so, ask him if he remembers when Messina left the table. I want you to call on the owner of the restaurant that did the catering. Here's the info," Travis said as he got up and handed a business card to Ramón.

"What line of questioning should I pursue with him?"

"I need to know about the couple he hired to serve. Get any background info and whatever else you can find out about the timing of everything. Also, find out about the guy that brought in the large utensils later. Talk to the captain first, though. He wants you in on a search for the murder weapon. Oh, and by the way, call the restaurant owner at home; I don't think they're open for lunch, so I don't expect him to be at the restaurant on a Sunday morning."

Ramón nodded and headed for the conference room.

Travis stepped into the waiting room. Mike Kreissman hadn't arrived yet, giving him a chance to check in with Julia. As usual, she managed the case from the office and hopefully had more info on the victim. Her research was essential in all his cases, and he hoped that something in Mr. Messina's past might give him a hint about a motive.

"Morning," he said as Julia looked up. "Thanks for putting in some extra time in today. Anything new?"

She was wearing a light sleeveless summer dress with a deep décolleté. Her auburn colored hair was pulled back into a ponytail. She smiled and rested her chin on her hands after she'd positioned her elbows on her desk.

"Nothing more than what we already know. I can't find anything before 2002, and it seems like Carlo paid his taxes on time."

Travis nodded slowly, thinking about what else she looked into today. Julia was the detectives' online specialist. She researched technical information, something in which most of the older detectives had no experience. He liked Julia's fast and dedicated work. "Bank accounts?"

"Checking into that."

"Good, also don't forget to check neighboring states. Maybe something will turn up."

Julia turned back to her screen. "Okay, I'll let you know what I find." She peered over his shoulder, and Travis looked back. An officer motioned for him to go back to the waiting room.

On his way, Travis stopped into the conference room. He refilled his cup while staring at the empty couch where he'd seen O'Hara ten minutes earlier. He hoped Kreissman would be more forthcoming.

Chapter 8

The Caterer

The call lasted all of a few minutes as the restaurant owner told Ramón to meet him at the place of business on Falls of the Neuse in twenty minutes. Ramón wondered why the man couldn't just answer a few simple questions on the phone. He shrugged and walked out to his car. Already a bit disappointed that he didn't see Mr. O'Hara anywhere, he now had to travel to North Raleigh.

The late morning drive was smooth, and by ten, he got to Pierro's Trattoria, in the corner of a shopping strip. The sign on the door said *Closed*, so he knocked on the door. He vaguely heard a voice inside and was able to make out that someone was coming.

The door appeared to be unlocked, and the owner shook hands with Ramón. "Come in, come in, please. I'm Pierro Pirelli. How ya doin?"

Ramón took off his hat. "Ramón Acosta."

"Sure, sure. Let's go into the kitchen, come," Pierro said as he led the way. At first, the kitchen looked a little messy, but as

Ramón walked further, he realized that everything seemed organized.

"Espresso?" Pierro asked. Not waiting for an answer, he grabbed the portafilter's metal handle and cleaned it out by hitting it over an open bin. He filled it with grounds of a brand of coffee Ramón had never seen. Once the basket was full, Pierro applied some pressure on the top to ensure a more robust flavor and jammed it in the machine between the water reservoir and the two spouts below.

Ramón nodded as Pierro grabbed two small cups from a shelf and placed each of them under a spout. Once he pressed a button, the machine started making noise, and coffee started flowing.

"So, Mr. Pirelli, I'm here to discuss the catering your restaurant did last night at Carolina Arbors."

"Sure, I understand. Eh, quite some story there, no? They killed one of the guests, right?"

"Yes, and..."

"Listen," Pierro interrupted. "Our food is good. We didn't poison the guy, you know," Pierro laughed.

"No, that's not what I was going to say. I just wanted to talk about your people who served the food."

The machine had quieted down, and the last drops fell from the spouts. Pierro took both cups and put them on a table. "Sugar?"

"No, thank you," Ramón said.

Pierro put two spoons of sugar in his cup and stirred it. "Come, let's go outside, man. I need a cigarette."

Ramón took his cup and took a sip. He grimaced, tasting the strong coffee, and almost put it down, ready to walk away. He reconsidered as he didn't want to offend Pierro. Sticking his cap under his left arm, he followed Pierro and held the delicate cup in his right hand. The small landing outside couldn't have been more than twelve square feet.

"As I was asking," Ramón continued. "What can you tell me about your people serving the food last night?"

"Hey, they're good friends of mine. They live in the neighborhood there. I was short-staffed, and I asked them to help out setting the table. I had Uber-eats deliver the food, the dishes, and utensils: Appetizer, a main dish, and of course, tiramisu for dessert."

"So, your people weren't even there."

"Right. Too busy here."

"But one of your men went out after all, right?"

"Oh yes, now I remember. The driver had forgotten the box with the serving spoons. Yeah, I lost a waiter for almost an hour." Pierro took one more sip of his coffee and took a long drag of his cigarette.

"Okay, but what can you tell me about that waiter?"

"He's a good man and worked here for over ten years."

"What's his name?"

"Antonio, Ragosta. We call him Tony."

"I see. When did Tony leave here?"

"I think we got the call from my friends around six-fifteen, and he left right away."

"What time do you estimate he returned?"

Pierro took one last drag from his cigarette and tossed the smoldering rest in a small bucket hanging from the railing. "He was back in an hour as I said, so I'd say at seven-fifteen."

Knowing the timeline so far, Ramón realized that Tony couldn't be involved since, at the time of the murder, he was already back at the restaurant. As they walked back into the kitchen, José, the chef, was already working on a lunch catering job. He waved hello and continued working. Once in the seating area, Ramón asked: "And regarding those friends of yours. Do you know them well?"

"Sure, sure. They've been coming here for many years."

"It sounds like quite a job, serving sixteen people. Have they ever done that before?"

"No, the first time. Last week, I told them that I had a catering job in their neighborhood, and since I had two people sick, I called them to see if they could help out. They're great people, and I'm sure they did a great job."

"I heard they didn't get past the appetizer. What happened to the other food?"

"They kept it warm until about nine-thirty and then cleaned up. This morning, Tony picked it up and took it to a soup kitchen."

"I see. I guess it keeps that long."

"The Osso Bucco keeps well, and the tiramisu was already refrigerated. No problem."

"Just in case the detective didn't ask your friends, but perhaps you have their telephone number?"

"I guess that would be okay. Wait here, and I'll get the number."

Ramón waited patiently, looking around the restaurant seating area with all white linen-covered tables. He thought it might be rather an expensive place, but when he picked up a menu from a small credenza, he checked the prices and was pleasantly surprised. He'd come here with his girlfriend perhaps. He checked out all the bottles of wine on display when Pierro returned.

"Here's their telephone number. I'm sure they'll tell you pretty much the same I told you."

"Thanks. Oh, and one more thing. Did the men's club that had their food catered, pay for the services?"

"It was pre-paid, including the tip."

"Who paid for it?"

"I believe it was a guy named Marc. Do you need a copy of the receipt?"

"I don't think so. Thanks for all your info. Maybe I'll stop by one day."

"Sure, always welcome," Pierro said and walked Ramón to the door.

Ramón took off in a hurry for Piedmont Hall. He was skeptical about finding the murder weapon, but the captain's orders prevailed, and lunch would have to wait.

Chapter 9

Bocce Ball

Three courts were in use at the Sunday morning bocce ball games in the back of the clubhouse. Bill and Phinn were late arrivals, hoping to get one game in, but had to wait their turn to replace the next team that lost. Phinn had only shown up to put his mind on something besides his interview fiasco with the detective. Bill wondered why Phinn was quiet but left the man to his thoughts. He figured that all the guys in the men's club were a little depressed. Bill and his wife had served the food, and after they talked briefly with the detective, they hadn't seen the men again.

It wasn't until Raja joined them that they rehashed the event from the previous evening. It started merely by Raja asking Phinn if indeed he'd been there last night. He continued: "And were you the one who found the body?"

Phinn hesitated. It was still all too raw for him, but as his therapist after his treatment by the mob had instilled in him, sometimes it is better to grab the bull by the horns and talk about what ails you. He took a deep breath and stood up. "I didn't find it, but I did see it. It was terrible."

"Like a lot of blood?" Raja wanted to know.

"No, just the body with the throat slit, leaning against one of the shower stalls."

"You mean in the one right there?" Raja asked, pointing to the downstairs entry. "Wow, that must have been something. Did you take any pictures?"

"Of course I didn't," Phinn shot back. It was bad enough that he would remember this scene and all other gruesome scenes he'd witnessed over the years. "What good would a picture do anyway?"

"Sorry, just wanted to check," Raja said in a more subdued voice. "Are they following any leads?"

"I don't think so," Phinn said, staring at one of the games where a set of balls were very close to the palenta. "I guess the detective in charge is still talking with possible witnesses."

"Did you see him again?" Bill asked.

"Yeah," this morning. That's why I was late. "Just told the detective what I knew and what I had seen."

Bill had been listening while watching the end of a game. "Hey, look!" he said. "Game over on the second court. Let's get your mind on something else." He tapped Phinn on the shoulder, and they both joined the winners.

Raja said hello to the men coming off the court. "You guys hear about the murder last night?"

They both nodded. "Phinn was one of the first to see the body."

One of the men had been drinking from his water bottle and looked surprised. "Really? I heard it was a guy named George who found him."

"I guess that's all part of the rumor mill around here," the second man offered.

"What's not a rumor is that I saw Bill the other day talking to a new resident. From what I saw on the news this morning, I'm sure he talked to the very fellow who got killed last night..."

"You mean to say that Bill is involved?" the first man asked.

"I didn't say that. Meeting someone isn't a crime, but Bill wasn't very forthcoming about it. That's all I'm saying."

"That's odd," the second man said. "I was talking to Bill yesterday afternoon. He told me that he was helping out catering dinner for that men's club. I think his wife was doing it too."

"You know what?" Raja said. "If you ask me, I'd tell you that both Bill and Phinn have something to hide. We haven't heard the last of this."

"Ah, c'mon Raja," the second man said. "Aren't you exaggerating a bit? These are good men. I think Phinn was a cop in NY City once."

"Where I come from, that's not worth much. A little bribe goes a long way. Anyway, just saying. You guys staying?"

"I've got to go," the first man said. "You can take my place in the next game."

Raja smiled. He knew that he would ask some more questions if he got the chance to play against Phinn or Bill. After all, Raja had been a prosecutor in Punjab forty years ago. He'd seen it all. He didn't tell any of the men that Carlo had been his neighbor for almost two weeks.

Chapter 10

Mike Kreissman

On his way over to the station, Mike was driving on automatic as he called it. No matter what was going on around him, or whatever thoughts infiltrated his mind, his driving was spot-on. Having been a New York cabbie will do that to you, he used to say. Not that he hadn't had his share of accidents, but some things just couldn't be avoided with tons of idiots driving in the city.

The events from last night brought some unforgettable memories back. He hardly ever thought about those few days in the city, but a tragedy close by always seemed to wake up the feelings that generally stayed subdued. He recalled how one day he was coming into LGA from visiting a friend in Houston. It was a beautiful sunny September day, and the plane glided across Jamaica Bay over the Twin Towers. His Mom always loved going there, and he'd made a promise to himself that when she was feeling better, he'd take her to dinner again at *Windows on the World*. She loved looking out over the city lights so much, and she almost forgot to eat dinner the last time they'd been there. *Mike, the bridges look like bracelets over the water,* she once said, always having a way with words. As he landed, he planned to take her to the restaurant again for her birthday. He loved doing things for her that she considered too expensive for her budget.

After unpacking in a pretty haphazard fashion, Mike had tucked into bed and listened to the sirens and usual city noises. He'd gotten a subsidized apartment at Mitchell-Lama on 79th and First Avenue. He considered himself lucky to live in the Yorkville area where he never felt unsafe on the street, no matter what time of night he got off the bus. Living on the 15th floor was okay with him. In an emergency or when the elevators didn't work, he could always climb up or down the stairs.

He remembered how the next morning, he faced another stressful day with a crazy morning rush hour. He never thought he would wind up driving a cab for a living and trying to make ends meet on such a small salary. It was hard trying not to have an accident in such a rushed society. Everyone was always in such a hurry to get where they needed to go. He often felt like telling his passengers to just set their alarm clock for a little earlier time, so they wouldn't have to rush around like a maniac. But you never knew what was going on in their lives, just like he never knew what would happen in his own life. It seemed that every few weeks, he had more demands for overdue bills than he could ever remember. Things were more relaxed and simpler in North Carolina.

Coming to Highway 147 toward Durham this morning, he could barely merge. Traffic was almost a standstill. He checked the time on his console. Perhaps better late than never. He got into the right lane and resumed recalling the incredible event from that fateful day after his return from Texas, now almost twenty years ago.

After a fitful night, imagining all the noise and traffic to come, he'd given up on sleep, gotten out of bed, and showered. Grabbing a bagel out of the freezer, he popped it into the microwave and waited for the buzzer. He wrapped it in a paper towel and shoved it into his pocket. He walked to the garage that morning. Who knew, maybe the exercise would perk him up a bit. In September in New York, leaves started to turn, but it felt like an Indian summer was well on its way. He strode down First Avenue, enjoying the mild exertion. It didn't stop him from munching on his bagel, figuring he'd get some New York fuel into his system. From 79th Street, he walked west to Lexington, turned left, and down the seven blocks to the garage. He swiped his I.D. card, clocking him in, and went to get the keys for his cab. He appreciated that all cabs were non-smoking now. He never got used to the overpowering stale odor of tobacco.

He found his cab in the rank, an old Crown Victoria with over 200,000 miles on the odometer. Sighing, he wondered if his profit would be negated by the fuel costs of today's trips. Granted, some folks still loved the old sedans, comfortable riding to the end of their usefulness, like sitting on the living room couch. He vowed to stay under thirty-five all day.

Sitting in slow-moving traffic now on his way to downtown Durham, he clearly remembered that his first fare was a pickup around the corner, taking him all the way downtown to the South Tower. He'd figured Second Avenue might be a better bet than the FDR. His passenger had stepped in as he pulled to the curb and was already on his phone, giving buy and sell directions. As usual, Mike had his ears peeled for any useful stock info.

He'd made it downtown in record time, pulling up into the passenger area in front of the South Tower. For a change, the fare handed him $50 cash, for which he knew he didn't have change. Mike started to say that, but the fellow waved at him, smiled, and mouthed *Keep the change.*

He hoped it signaled the start of a great day. Unfortunately, quite the unimaginable opposite happened. Just as he'd gotten out of the car for a moment, watching the man walk into the building, he felt a sudden downward draft while hearing a deafening noise. He knew it wasn't a car crash; instead, it came from above. At a loss of what happened, he looked up in terror and saw flames shooting out of the North Tower. His first thought was about an enormous explosion up there. He didn't know what to do first, run far away from it if stuff started to fall, or keep watching.

By the time he'd composed himself a bit, people were already running out of the lobby as fiery debris indeed started hitting the ground. Mike jumped towards the building and began pulling people by the hand to get them away from falling ash, stone, and metal. A young woman just started screaming, standing stock still, looking upwards. Mike grabbed her arm and began pulling her across the street, heading to Trinity Church. He figured the further away they got, the safer they would be. As grey ash floated down over a wider area, it burned his eyes and got into his nose, making it suddenly hard to breathe. He kept pulling her as she screamed. The smell of kerosene was pervasive. He kept moving south and had his eye on the steeple for direction. People were running after them, and he wanted to make sure he had his bearings right. He never thought he would have the guts to help anyone besides himself and his Mom, but he made sure the folks followed him. Finally, he saw the door, and all he kept thinking was to run and run until safely inside! One push, and he and the girl got inside the back portal of the church. Then, he held the door and guided people inside.

He knew there were other people on the street, so he ran out and kept directing people to the open door. The priests and church employees came out and assisted running people too. He took a white handkerchief out of his pocket, tied it around his head, covering his mouth and nose, and ran back up Church Street to help a few more folks find Trinity. That was one of the things he remembered for sure of the day. There'd been so many terrified people who needed help. When the stream of people stopped, he went back to the tower to find his cab. Just as he got in, two things happened. First, there was another loud noise, not unlike the first one. He looked up but could only see smoke. He saw people pointing at the South Tower. He stepped out of his cab for a better look when people ran out of that tower's lobby within a minute. A man with his face partially bloodied ran to the taxi, his clothes covered in fine white dust. The stranger jumped in the back seat and yelled, "Get the hell out of here!" He'd done just that and drove uptown via FDR, seeing hundreds of police cars and at least thirty fire engines coming from the opposite direction. At one point, there were no more cars. He pulled over and got out, looking back at the carnage. His ride jumped out and disappeared. Somehow, Mike hadn't cared.

Mike pulled into the parking lot of the police station in Durham. He dabbed his eyes with a tissue, having thought again about that fateful day for perhaps the hundredth time.

While Julia dove into more records on Carlo, Travis collected the next member of the quartet. He saw Mike blowing his nose as he walked into the waiting room.

"Mr. Kreissman. I was waiting for you," Travis said. "Please follow me."

There wasn't any coffee left in the conference room, and Travis suggested a glass of water. He noticed that Mr. Kreissman looked a bit upset, eyes red, and slightly out of breath. Perhaps a restless night, he figured.

"A glass of water would be fine," Mike answered and sat down.

Once two glasses were on the table, Travis started with small talk, guessing that perhaps this man needed to be put at ease. "Lots of traffic this morning?"

"Usually not on 147," Mike said. "Today was a bit of an exception with two lanes closed after nine. Sorry if I'm late."

"No problem," Travis smiled. "Thanks for coming in."

"Yes, I guess you needed to follow up on your questioning of last night."

"Yes. We'll get to that," Travis said, leaning back comfortably while Mike still sat hunched over, holding the glass of water with both hands.

"Had a rough night, knowing that you lost one member of your quartet?"

"Nothing upsets me more than seeing people suffer or get killed for no apparent reason," Mike answered after taking a big gulp of water. "We'd just met the guy, for Christ's sake, and then he gets killed?"

"I'm sure it's upsetting," Travis said the obvious. "Did you have someone to talk to last night when you got home?"

"Yeah, sure. My wife was still up watching one of those soapy predictable Hallmark movies. She paused the TV to get the whole story. So yeah, we talked for a while."

"Good," Travis said. "I don't have too many questions for you, actually, the obvious ones and some of them I already asked last night, but this time I may have to take notes."

"That's okay," Mike said, sitting back a bit, crossing his right leg over his left knee.

"So, before last night, you had never met Mr. Carlo Messina?"

Right away, Travis saw the hesitation.

Mike pulled his leg more toward his body and almost emptied his lungs, pushing air out of his mouth. It made it evident that he didn't want to answer that question just yet. He'd purposely avoided thinking about that during the drive. Having chosen to recall the events of the morning of 9/11 seemed easier than thinking about the matter at hand. He took a deep breath.

"Did you, or didn't you?" Travis asked.

Mike looked up at the ceiling, slowly shaking his head. "It's weird," he said. "I don't know what to say."

"Oh, you're not sure you knew him before or weird answering a simple question?"

"It's complicated," Mike said, grabbing his elevated leg at his knee and ankle.

"Okay. Why don't you try to explain it to me? Maybe we can figure this out together. Give it a try."

"It's just that it was something that crossed my mind yesterday when I saw him at the dinner."

"What was that?"

"It's strange. So, my first answer to your question is: I didn't meet Carlo until yesterday."

"And the second?"

"I met him once before, a long time ago."

"How do you explain that one?"

"I was thinking about it this morning on the way over, but I'm not sure I'm correct. Between the awful day when the towers came down and the fact that I'm starting to forget things as they were sometimes, it's confusing getting old, you know what I mean, so, I have some doubts."

"What you're saying is that you think that at some point, you may have known or seen Mr. Messina, but you're unsure because of the circumstances in which you met?"

"That's about it," Mike said, uncrossing his legs. "Last night, when I saw him, I had an immediate feeling of recognition. I'm not sure it was likewise."

"Where do you think you met him before?"

"I probably wouldn't have given it a thought, but when Joe Malinski pointed him out to me yesterday while he was talking with O'Hara, something happened in my brain."

"What did Mr. Malinski say to warrant that?"

"The funny thing is, he's the forgetful one and sometimes confuses people with others. I think he's got the first signs of dementia if you ask me. Anyway, he said that this guy reminded him of a heavy thug he was once tracking in the city. I mean New York City."

"Did he say he recognized him, or did he look like someone?"

"Neither. Just reminded Malinski of someone."

"And what happened then?"

"When we walked over, I suddenly had the same feeling. It's amazing what the powers of suggestion will do to you."

"I get that. So, where did you possibly know the man from?"

"I'm going out on a limb here, detective," Mike answered. "It was the way the guy looked around in a strange environment. The eyes were set deep but confident. A bit of a smug look."

"And..."

"I remember seeing someone like that. It was just before the twin towers collapsed. He was coming out of the South Tower, all dusted up but not in a panic. He got into my taxi, and I took off. He never said where he wanted to go, and I never asked. All I wanted to do was to get away from that awful scene. I think he thought about it the same way, you see. Who wouldn't have that day?"

"So, you remember him as your ride that day?"

"I'm still not sure, but I can't stop thinking about it. You can imagine why I hesitated to say something. I mean, that was so long ago. I only consider it a possibility because I clearly remember a young woman that I lead to the nearby church to keep her safe. I still see her face and the faces of many others that followed us that day to a safe place. I didn't want to stay there since I was concerned about my mother, you see. I was lucky to find my cab and get away from the place. So, yes, I do remember people's faces, and I think he was my last ride that day."

Chapter 11

Carlo Messina

Julia had been at her desk all morning. Her attempts to find anything about Carlo Messina on social media sites were a bust. Others with the same name didn't match any of the scarcity of information she already had. She had a long way to go, but searching the old fashioned way always turned up something. With access to tri-state databases, she started with known residences. She quickly found his last known address in Jersey City, New Jersey. There was still a listing for him on Logan Avenue in the West End of the city. Updates usually took months, and many search engines would forever keep previous addresses as part of the person's background. It indicated his age as sixty, but looking for a birth certificate without knowing where he was born was a little premature. She jotted down his birth year as most likely being 1960.

She moved on to more accessible financial data using his address and quickly found confirmation of Carlo's single bank account. He banked with Conglomerate Bank. Checking out the bank, she was surprised it was more of a bank for businesses with many overseas transactions. His account was active, and she was able to take a look at it. She noticed monthly deposits from a company called Hospitality Services. She wasn't able to look back more than a year, but at least she had a link to an existing company. She wrote down the name while she continued checking out the bank. It turned out that the institution had been under investigation for money laundering, was accused at one time of having ties to criminal elements in the U.S. and abroad, and had links with shady banks in South America. Those banks, in turn, had links to drug cartels. There were several articles about the bank, and she printed out most of it for the file and Vinder's eyes only.

In her simple Google search, Julia had also seen Carlo's name linked to a Ramada Inn in Jersey City. A few calls later, she had confirmation: the man had worked at the hotel from 2002 until he quit in 2017. She figured that's when he went to work for another company. There was nothing listed before 2002 and her call to Hospitality Services went nowhere. Nobody picked up, and there was no possibility to leave a message.

Julia checked the time and decided to call the sales office at Carolina Arbors to follow up on Ramón's visit. A message redirected her to a location off-site as their sales center had been closed. She was lucky to find someone there on a Sunday morning and quickly found the closing attorney's information. The follow-up call would have to wait until Monday. From the salesperson, she learned that Mr. Messina had paid cash for the Castle Rock style house. He was also the single buyer and confirmed what Ramón had already surmised. Carlo may indeed have been alone when he died, but Julia looked for divorce records. No official records in the states of New York and New Jersey popped up for either a wedding or a divorce. It bothered her that there was nothing before 2002 and that Travis would be disappointed. She looked at the half-page of notes and shook her head. Travis' cases hinged a lot on knowing the victim and his or her story. He told her several times that motive was always guided by things in the past, sometimes across generations, regardless of whether the underlying basis was revenge, money, or jealousy. She took a break and retrieved the printed article on Conglomerate Bank.

Back at her desk, she stapled her handwritten notes to the printout and decided to give Hospitality Services another ring. This time she was able to leave a message. She stressed the urgency of returning her call on her desk phone and provided Travis's mobile number.   A more in-depth search on the company had better results when she found a link between them and the bank. The company provided hospitality services. They supplied personnel responsible for first contacts with clients, identifying the need for services at the bank, such as enforcing the uttermost cleanliness to all rooms, janitorial services, food delivery for events, regulating building access, and so on. She wondered at what level Mr. Messina had functioned. While she added some of the information to the top sheet for Travis, she assumed a return call would resolve that.

Chapter 12

Joe Malinski

Vinder peered at the tall fit man sitting across from him and felt a bit embarrassed. It was unusual that someone was excited to talk to a Durham detective. No caginess, no wall at all. Joe Malinski, obviously a lifelong runner, had the bearing and energy of a man decades younger than the seventy-three years Travis gathered from his driver's license.

"Hi Joe," Travis started in his usual way. "How long have you lived at the Arbors?"

"Just about three years now. Quite a change from before, but we do like it."

Vinder knew that Joe was in his element and could be a big help. Torn between establishing himself as either a colleague or an interrogator, he thought, *Crap, this guy knows all the tricks. There's isn't a choice. Brother-in-arms is it, then.*

"Joe," Travis started. "As you know, I asked you to come in today because I had a few more questions, given the incomplete investigation last night. Anything you may have found out that may help us in the Carlo Messina case?"

Joe leaned forward, drew his brows in, and sat low in his chair with his shoulders drooping low. It appeared to Vinder that he was traveling back in time. Then he started to speak.

"The short answer is *No*, detective. The long answer requires me to tell you a bit about me and my life, so you understand what I am mean by that."

"No problem," Travis smiled. "I like some background. As a retired detective yourself, you've experienced a lot, I'm sure." He poured two glasses of water and put one in front of Joe. "I'm listening."

Joe took a sip from the glass and sat up a bit. "As you know, I'm retired NYPD. I started on patrol in Brooklyn, particularly in Flatbush. Flatbush was an Italian, Irish, and Jewish neighborhood in the late '60s when I started. The streets smelled of oregano and chicken soup, and the mamas kept them clean. In the 80's it changed. Now it smells like Jamaican jerk and Callaloo." He took another sip. Travis sat back and steeled himself for a long conversation. Joe continued, "I was assigned to the Street Crimes Unit in '73 and stayed there until the late eighties when my fair complexion made it difficult to gain the trust of the Caribbean community. But, from the seventies, I built great relationships with the people in the neighborhood. I joined Our Lady of Refuge on Foster, and it was good to be close with many of the families there. It's a very pretty little church with a lovely garden and a craftsman, art deco vibe."

Travis wasn't drinking at all. He was wondering where Joe was going with all that. How did all this tie to the case at hand? He didn't even know what to say or ask at this point. Perhaps, he figured, a little direction would make Joe focus on why he was here today. "I'm sure it is," Travis said. "Now, how about your take on the murder? You mentioned last night that you met up with Mr. Messina last week. Perhaps you can elaborate a little on that."

"That's what I'm getting to," Joe said. "To explain my take on this and my meeting with Carlo, I need to go back a while, you see."

"Okay, Joe, go ahead," Travis said with some trepidation because it could take some time for the story to come out.

"Let me jump forward then. You see, I have a little "trait" that you'll probably hear about and will most likely impact how you think about what I'm telling you. A few years ago, I had a series of transient ischemic attacks or mini-strokes. A great vascular surgeon at Mt. Sinai operated on my carotids and fixed me right up, but it left me with an annoying habit of mistaking people I meet now with those I knew in the past. It drives me right out of my mind since I was always known for never forgetting a face. I guess I still don't forget the old ones, but I can't seem to learn new faces. They kinda morph together like that app on phones."

"Wow, I'm sorry about that. It must be hard for you, but I also think you remember your days on the beat very well."

"That I do. I want to go back to Flatbush, though. Then, as now, the boys in Flatbush formed gangs. I guess boys are just that way. In privileged neighborhoods, they'd join the boy scouts. In Flatbush, you either were an altar boy, or you joined a gang. Sometimes both. Even the Jews had gangs."

Travis nodded, opened his notebook but remained quiet.

"These gangs weren't like today," Joe continued. "Drugs hadn't flooded the streets yet. Mostly they were kids that hung together and got into some trouble. I remember one group that thought it was hilarious to use slingshots and ball bearings to break car windows. Unfortunately, they decided to attack a row of Cadillacs with black mirrored windows one night. The idiots didn't realize that those were local mobsters' cars. When the glass started breaking, the gumbos ran out, weapons drawn, and the kids ran off and hid in the local cemetery. I don't think they did that again!'" Joe swigged the last of the water.

"Not if they wanted the mob on their butts," Travis chuckled.

"That's another thing: the mob. For context, Flatbush is close to Park Slope, where most of the top guys lived. Capone lived there once upon a time. Either there or in Williamsburg, which is a few miles north. Flatbush had a bunch of the mid-level guys living there. The enforcers, drivers, and button men. I don't know who did more to keep the streets safe back then, the police or the mob. They certainly didn't allow any nonsense around their houses. Now, some of the Italian kids had a romantic idea of becoming "made" men. They gravitated to a particularly violent gang who all had this small capital letter U-shaped tattoo above their left wrist. It looked more like sharp bull horns. I seem to remember them calling themselves the Torellos."

Vinder took note and doodled a bit with the letter U while Joe carried on.

'These kids ran numbers and made collections for the mob. They robbed the Jewish shopkeepers and the Irish pub owners. There was one particular kid who seemed to enjoy beating people. He was about ten years younger than me and good looking. Strong with black curly hair and big brown eyes. He looked like an angel and charmed the pants off many a young lady, but he was dark. I jammed him up a couple of times, but the lawyers always got him out except for the last time. He was a suspect in a cop killing, and rumor had it that he'd started to collect for himself. I imagine the mob wasn't happy with that one. Anyway, I lost track of him. The neighborhood was changing fast by then, and the Italians moved on. I heard that the cops brought him in on some RICO charges in the late nineties. Don't know what happened."

Travis was still waiting patiently, hoping to hear the connection. "So, things changed in the eighties and nineties, and I get that. Coming back to the case last night, I wonder if any of this is related."

Joe sat up straight, resting both hands on the table. "That's what I'm getting at. You see, that punk disappeared from my radar for years, that is, until I met Carlo last week at Piedmont Hall. I told you last night that Marc had asked me to meet with him over a week ago. The poolroom seemed to be a good place to get together, and I set up a meeting. He was playing pool all alone when I walked in. Involuntarily, perhaps because of my disease, I started by saying: "Gino, what are you doing here?" He just stared at me, and I may have imagined it, but he seemed to recognize me. He quickly corrected me and said his name was Carlo, not Gino, and turned his back to take another shot. We talked for a while, explained some things about the men's club and the rules. He said he was from New Jersey, and we talked a little about that area. He seemed friendly and forthcoming. He'd lived there his whole life, and after a while, I was becoming convinced that I had morphed someone else again. It happens all the time now." Joe sat back as if signaling that he finished and there was nothing more to say.

"So, seeing him last night, did it confirm that you knew Carlo from before?"

"No, it didn't at all. It was as if I had straightened things out in my head, and I was no longer confused."

"You didn't bring it up with anyone else?"

"About my confusion? Hell no. What would the members be thinking?"

"How about mentioning the name Gino to the other guys in your quartet, Mike and Phinn?"

"I don't recall, detective," Joe said, putting his arms on the side of the chair, ready to push himself up.

"Okay, noted. If you think of anything else that might give us some clues in the case, call me. You know where to find me," Travis said, unsure he wanted this conversation to be over.

"Will do," Joe said and got up.

Chapter 13

The Murder Weapon

Ramón made it back to the clubhouse on time and walked straight to the back of the building. He kept his hat on to shield the sun from hitting his eyes. He didn't often wear sunglasses, but today's harsh sun pierced mercilessly through the canopy of an intense Carolina blue sky, making them necessary. It was almost noon, and the only people he could see sat near the pool. The yellow tape near the entrance to the locker room had been removed. A sign on the brown door announced that the place was still off-limits. He figured that management hired a cleaning company, judging by the paint buckets and cleaning products sitting outside the propped open door. From what he'd seen the evening before, they indeed needed to do a deep cleaning of the inside. He walked away from the building and scanned the area. His gaze went from the path coming down to the outside pool area, across the bocce ball courts, further to his right and the tennis courts. He checked the time and made a quick call.

"How far are you out?"

He listened briefly and hung up. It was hot standing on the concrete surface, and for a moment, the pool looked like a better place to be. He decided to wait in the shade near the outside double set of concrete stairs. He hadn't volunteered to search for the murder weapon, but here he was. Earlier in the morning, the captain had told him that Officer Duff was to take the lead at noon. Apparently, Duff had a knack for figuring out where criminals ditched their weapons. Ramón had resisted knowing it would be a futile outside activity. He argued with the captain, saying that the killer never left the room through the outer door, implying that it was unlikely that the murder weapon would turn up there. The captain overruled his single objection. Perhaps one way to prove his hunch was to join in the search. After all, who said the murder weapon was ditched.

Officer Duff had gone into the building through the front entrance since he appeared on the back stairs leading to the recreational area. Ramón saw the rather heavy-set officer as he reached the sidewalk. Duff was already sweating, and his crew cut blond hairdo seemed to glow in the sun. Ramón waived him on toward the shower room and into the shade.

"Ramón," he said and shook hands with the officer.

Duff nodded. "The crime scene?".

"Yes. Forensics has released it, and I'm sure those guys went through everything."

"I saw the pictures."

"Oh, good," Ramón answered as they entered.

Duff walked to the wall on his left. "So this is where they discovered traces of blood spatter. I checked with the coroner's office, and they're pretty sure it was a very sharp knife, judging by the clean-cut."

"I know they checked all the garbage cans, and nothing turned up."

"Probably ditched outside," Duff said, turning around.

"That's the problem," Ramón said. "There's no record of anyone coming out of this room after the murder."

"I believe you, but the perp could've gone upstairs and then outside, backtracking to where there are no cameras."

"Possibly, but I don't see why he'd do that."

"Well, let's go over a possible path he might have taken."

"So, we go through that door over there," Ramón said, pointing to the door leading to the Varsity Room.

Duff glanced briefly at the rest of the men's locker room and walked out.

"Most likely, he took these stairs on the left to make his way upstairs," Ramón said. "Going through the room where they were having dinner doesn't make sense."

"I agree, but how about the area to the right?"

"As you can see, a few vending machines and the room with the mirrors, referred to as the Cardinal Room. We checked all of that, including the space behind the machines."

"How about furniture?"

"Not sure. Do you want to check it?"

Duff nodded and started to turn over the seats. Nothing seemed cut or removed, and there was no space to slide in a knife. "How about the women's locker room."

"Haven't been in there," Ramón said. "Not sure forensics went through it."

"Let's start here," Duff said.

Ramón opened the door and called out to see if anyone was inside. Getting no response, they both entered. The layout was a mirror image of the men's room. Duff glanced up and down, checked behind toilets, peeked inside the water tanks, and under the counters. He briefly checked the area on top of the lockers.

"I need to check every locker."

"I'm not sure there's a master key. I can check with our technicians if they've already done this search."

"Sure. It might save us some time."

Ramón made the call and talked very briefly to one of the team members. He hung up and nodded. "Yes, they went through every single locker, but they didn't go into the Cardinal Room."

"In that case, let's take a look in there," Duff said, seemingly in a hurry as he bolted for the open doors. He scanned the room briefly, shaking his head. "Not a place to hide a knife. Outside it is then," he said and headed for the stairs.

They came up near the front desk. Duff, a little out of breath, stopped and stared at the camera on the ceiling. "Tapes were checked, I assume?"

"Yes, they were. Detective Vinder and I did," Ramón confirmed. "We saw the man who had entered the locker room downstairs leave much later. All he had was a towel over his shoulder. He still wore his bathing suit, a T-shirt, and a baseball cap. We also know that he wasn't who he was supposed to be. This man may have looked like someone from this neighborhood, and he might have used that person's key card. Travis is working on that."

Duff put his hands on his hips and kept looking around. "I still think he walked out with that knife. Perhaps a folding knife. Which would be easy to hide under a cap or in a pocket."

"He could've taken it with him as well..." Ramón offered.

"Small chance. To me, this crime looks like a hit. In most cases, the murderer ditches the weapon after cleaning it to remove fingerprints. I'd say we take a look in the parking lot." Duff took a deep breath and walked outside into the hot air.

Ramón followed him to the large flower pots near the entrance.

Duff poked a small rod he produced from his pocket into the dirt. "Also, in my experience, the weapon is ditched quickly at an unusual place." He looked over the parking lot and started to walk toward the pickleball courts. When seeing the small concrete roofless building between the courts and the clubhouse, he stood still. "Aha," he smiled. "A perfect place."

The small structure had an opening on one side. A large dumpster with the top removed sat in the middle of the enclosed area. The sliding panel on the dumpster was in the open position. Some old folding chairs and broken furniture crammed the right of the dumpster. To the left, a discarded metal large birdhouse with several nesting openings straddled several bent traffic signs. Ramón thought the birdhouse looked more like an apartment for birds. The pole that held the birdhouse was bent severely, rendering it practically useless.

"Help me in the dumpster," Duff said, grabbing a broken office chair. Ramón held it steady, and Duff climbed in. "I bet it's here somewhere," he said and rummaged through cardboard boxes, metal scraps, and a pile of nets. "While I go through all this, why don't you check the pile with the signs."

Ramón started to pry open the small compartments in the birdhouse, but all were empty except for some dirt and feathers. He moved the bottom of the long pole near the bent area to check under the traffic signs but spotted a dirty cloth stuffed in the bottom of the rod. He looked around for something to pry it out since his fingers couldn't reach the plugged tube. "Hey, Duff," he yelled out. Something's strange here. Do you have that little rod handy?"

Duff poked his head through the opening in the dumpster and handed Ramón the small tool. "What'd you find?"

"A plugged pole. Need to get that out."

"Go ahead," Duff said, wiping his forehead with his sleeve as he dove back into the dumpster.

Ramón was able to loosen the cloth until a tip peeked out a bit. He slowly pulled it out and threw it to the side. He looked inside the opening and was disappointed to see nothing but darkness. He rotated the whole birdhouse construction such that the end of the bent part was facing down. He shook that part and, with a piece of wood, hit the side. That's when the knife fell out.

"Bingo," he yelled, staring at a brand-new plane-blade Buck *Slim-pro* folding knife with an oversized brown handle.

Chapter 14

Mr. Messina's Home

Travis found Julia's notes on his keyboard. He reached in the bottom drawer of his desk and pulled out the sandwich he'd brought from home and took a big bite. Reading through the short report, he learned that Mr. Messina's life had about forty years of unaccountability. That, in itself, didn't bother him right away. The fact that the last twenty or so years didn't indicate a motive puzzled him. Travis spent less than a minute looking through the attached document. The bank and its legal complications in the past seemed irrelevant at this point. A hospitality service running a building wasn't uncommon. Many businesses contracted in-house management, and financial institutions in New York City often did. Several bank headquarters couldn't be bothered by those mundane tasks, and they gladly employed a service company for cleaning and other housekeeping tasks.

He was wondering, though, what exactly Mr. Messina did for the company. He'd deal with that when they called back tomorrow. Nothing else in Julia's notes stood out. Motive proved elusive unless there was some controversy involving the victim at the bank or the hospitality company. He looked at the time on his phone and grabbed his jacket. On the way out, he took a bottle of water. He'd be at Mr. Messina's home in less than twenty minutes.

Once in his car, he called Ramón. "How did it go? Any luck?"

"Yes. I left you a message a while ago."

"Sorry, I've been interrogating those men from the club, and I haven't checked my messages."

"Well, we believe we found the murder weapon. It was hidden inside a metal rod in the garbage area at the clubhouse."

"What kind of knife was it?"

"A folded hunting knife."

"Do you still have it?"

"No, Duff took it straight to the lab. I'm still here because I ran into Mrs. Beaumont. I'm sure you remember her."

"How could I not. Don't tell me she had something to say about our case."

"As a matter of fact, she did. She couldn't talk because she had to join her water buddies in the pool. She'll finish around two o'clock. Any chance you can meet her here?"

"I'm on my way to the victim's house. I want to go through a few of those unpacked boxes we saw last night. Meet me there, and we'll deal with Charlotte afterward."

Ramón waited until Travis showed up at the house. There was an official note on the door, warning that the property was part of an investigation, and no trespassing was allowed.

Travis showed up, key in hand, and unlocked the door. "Let's tackle the few boxes in the bedroom first."

Ramón nodded and took out his phone. "Here, I took a few pictures of the knife." He held his phone in front of Travis as they walked to the ground floor bedroom."

"Had it been cleaned?"

"Yes, wiped clean, but perhaps not thorough enough. We should hear from the lab in a little while."

"Fingerprints would be nice, but unlikely that they'll find something. I'm convinced it was a professional hit."

The bedroom door stood wide open. The bed appeared carelessly made, but tidy enough for a bachelor. Two suitcases sat on a small dresser, and in a corner, several stacked cardboard boxes were still taped. Travis took out a pair of blue latex gloves from his back pocket. "Let's start with the suitcases. You take the black one," he nudged in the direction of the dresser.

Ramón also put gloves on, grabbed the suitcase, put it on the bed, and unzipped it. Travis did the same on the other side of the bed.

"Didn't forensics go through this?" Ramón asked.

"They did, but they only looked for letters and such addressed to the victim."

"Why? Were they in a hurry?"

"We went on a hunch that there may have been threatening letters perhaps. Anyway, they found nothing, and there hasn't been any time to go through the boxes in the garage. Most of them contained household items anyway. Make sure you check zipped pockets."

"Will do. What are we looking for?"

"Anything that will tell us something about Mr. Messina's past. I don't expect to find school reports, but anything that has to do with his jobs, banking, or travels. Preferably something more than twenty years ago."

"Okay. Well, nothing here so far," Ramón said as he returned clothing to the suitcase. He'd checked the lining for any hint of something hidden, but nothing felt suspicious. The zipped compartments were empty.

"Nothing here either," Travis said, putting his hands on his hips.

Ramón picked up the suitcase, and as he grabbed the handle, he noticed the tattered luggage tag. The plastic protector had become opaque. He opened the small buckle and examined it up close. "Got some paper in here," he said, starting to wrest the little card from the tag.

"This one doesn't have one," Travis said and walked around to Ramón's side.

Ramón took out the card and realized there were two cards. He showed the top one to Travis, who nodded. The address in Jersey City was the same Julia had written down. The second card was much older, with two corners ripped.

"Let me see that," Travis said. He looked at the handwritten address.

"Brooklyn," Ramón said.

"118 Clymer Street. No name"

"Lived there before, perhaps?"

"It's possible. This suitcase looks pretty old. It could've been someone else's. Call it in to Julia."

Ramón talked with her while Travis took the top box to the bed. Most of the contents were travel brochures. Pretty old, he figured. He wondered whether the victim traveled to those destinations in South America. He leafed through the small booklets, but no papers stuck inside. There were a few programs from Broadway performances. One was a *Blood Brothers* show on April 14, 1993.

"I don't know what Blood Brothers are all about, but that's for Julia to figure out later. Not sure it even matters or if it's of significance."

I'll start on the next box," Ramón said after he had bagged the booklet together with the luggage tag and cards.

The second box contained more clothes, and he tossed it aside quickly. The third box had a thin empty briefcase, advertising brochures from Hospitality Services, and a small women's wallet. Travis unzipped it right away, seeing pictures of children. They were all visible behind a clear plastic window. Where he would expect credit cards, there were three pictures of adults. He took all photos out and flipped them, but none had any writing on the back. Ramón laid them all out and looked intently at the faces. Two baby pictures were in black and white, and three pictures of young children were in color, but the quality was low. The images of adults were not as grainy.

Travis unzipped an inside pocket. He had some trouble with his latex gloves trying to pry out pieces of paper from the pocket. Slowly, a faint yellow folded sheet appeared.

"What do we have here?" he mumbled.

Ramón leaned closer.

Travis put the piece of paper on the bed and checked out the remainder of the wallet. There was nothing else left.

"Okay, this is odd," he said as he started to unfold the paper. "This looks like an old wallet and those pictures... I think the ones of the little children seem to be from the sixties." He continued unfolding until he was able to lay it flat on the bed. Once he did that, he saw right away that they dealt with a significant find.

"Perfect. A birth certificate and exactly what I was looking for," Travis said.

"Our victim's and that gets us way past what we got so far!" Ramón agreed. "Why don't we call this one in to Julia?"

Travis nodded and took a picture with his phone. A few taps later, the image was sent. As Ramón was folding the paper again, the phone rang. Travis answered, putting the conversation on speaker.

"Yes, don't tell me you already processed it."

"I'm not that fast," Julia said. "Anyway, now that we know that he was born in Scranton, Pa. and the birth date fits what I had already figured, I can do some targeted searches. I hadn't looked at records in that state, but I can get to it. Where did you ever find that?"

"In what I think is a woman's wallet. One of those old ones with a clasp."

"Any name, most likely the mother's name?"

"None. However, we do have some pictures."

"Well, what are you waiting for, Travis? Take a pic and shoot them over to me. By the time you get back here, I'll know a lot more."

"Snapping the photos now," Ramón said. "We do have some more boxes to go through. Also, we're meeting someone at the clubhouse first before coming in."

"Take your time," Julia said and ended the call.

Travis grabbed the last box in the room while Ramón bagged the pictures and the wallet. He cleared the rest of the contents of the previous boxes away from the bed. This box was heavier than the previous ones. He pulled out a small stuffed bear and handed it to Ramón. "Here, this is an old one. Probably older than you are."

Ramón chuckled a bit, shaking his head and put the toy on the bed. Travis handed him a wooden train engine. Most of the red and black colors had faded, and tiny pieces had chipped off. Below that, wrapped in a blue cloth, he found a heavy metal figurine of a cowboy on a horse. It looked like one of those bronze sculptures by Remington. Totally fake. He checked the bottom marble base, and it had a golden-colored sticker on it with the address of a Trophy Shop in Scranton.

"He sure got some nice toys when he was young," Ramón remarked as he put the toys on the bed.

"There's more here," Travis agreed. "This is a set of wooden blocks. An old puzzle. Each side of a block has part of a picture of an animal on it."

"I wonder why he kept these old worthless things."

"Assuming they're his, I don't know. It's not worth anything. Even that horse thing is a knock-off. The sentimental value, I guess," Travis answered. He pulled out a set of heavy skillets, barely used. There was a blue baby blanket, smelling of mothballs, and he gingerly handed it to Ramón. "I don't think there are any roaches in here, but check it."

Ramón took the blanket and shook it outside. Nothing fell out. On his way back in, he checked the label and noticed the hand-stitched name: Carlo. "Clean, and it belonged to Carlo, all right."

"I figured that already. The rest of the stuff in the box is small stuff. That's it for the bedroom. Let's go to the garage."

Chapter 15

Charlotte's Concern

The boxes in Carlo's garage didn't produce any evidence that might be useful in the investigation. Travis and Ramón were sure that Julia would shed some more critical light on Mr. Messina's life now that they had the birth certificate. They drove straight to the clubhouse where Charlotte Beaumont was waiting on a comfortable sofa in the foyer.

Travis thought about the night before when the place appeared jammed with people, most perhaps reluctant to talk, yet not part of the crime. He was almost sure that the killer had not been among them, but he did have a gut feeling that at least one person from the men's club knew more than they had shared with him. Seeing Charlotte, Travis took a deep breath, reflecting on her role in the murder of Mr. Kaufman over a year ago. How could he forget her witness statement in the Taco Truck murder six months ago? This lady was full of surprises, and as he walked up to her, she rose with a big smile.

"Good afternoon, Detective Vinder," she said, holding on to her bag overflowing with a huge colorful beach towel.

"Hello," Travis said, extending his hand. "Mrs. Beaumont, I hear from Officer Acosta you may be of help in our investigation."

Charlotte didn't shake hands and looked at both men. "Flu season is never over, detective. Y'all should be careful."

"Right you are," Travis said, sitting down across from her. "So, what can you tell us?"

"Well, let me go back, oh, I guess about a week."

"Sure, we're listening," Travis said, nodding toward Ramón, still standing. Ramón sat down next to him.

"So, I was at the pool here, having just enjoyed my morning dip, and I sat on one of the chairs. The weather was perfect, sunny, and cool. Now, as you know, I've lived in the South all of my life. I often found the summer heat almost unbearable. I'm just like those Yankees that are always moving down here. You know, I often chuckle when I think that my new neighborhood could replace Cary as the Containment Area for Relocated Yankees, except for size."

Travis didn't need to look at Ramón to know that he was rolling his eyes. Charlotte continued undisturbed.

"Anyway, I'd picked up a murder mystery book, but instead of reading it, I glanced around and noticed a gentleman that I didn't know and who reclined only a few seats to my left. We were alone at the pool. I was sure that I'd never met the man and that he was one of the 'new people.' Automatically acting on the manners drilled into me by my sweet Southern Mama, I considered it both my duty and my pleasure to welcome him to the neighborhood."

"I see," Travis said, having no idea where all this was leading. "So, how did that go?"

"I simply said *hello*, and *isn't it a beautiful day*, but a gruff 'yes' was his only reply. But you know me. My interest was instantly piqued. Was he unfriendly or only shy? A challenge to find out, no doubt. So, not deterred, I asked him if he was new to our neighborhood," she answered.

"What did he say?" Ramón asked.

"Well, the gentleman confirmed, with what I thought was a Brooklyn accent, that he'd moved in only two days ago," she replied. "I told him he was going to love it here. I told him about the many activities and clubs. I also asked him if he lived nearby. He mentioned the name of one of the newer streets near the entrance to the community. After I said that one of my dear acquaintances lived on that street, I told him my name."

Charlotte took a deep breath. Travis was still staring at a blank page in his notebook. Ramón had nudged himself into a corner of his seat and seemed relaxed as if Charlotte's story was slowly putting him to sleep.

"He said his name was Carlo, and suddenly showed a big smile and sparks of interest in his eyes. I felt the attraction but realized that it was too early to inquire about his marital status. However, I did reveal that I'd lived in North Carolina all my life. Anyway, Carlo moved to the seat next to me. He told me that he was originally from New York and had spent all of his life there. Now, detective, I noticed that he was rather handsome for his years, with some ethnic Italian heritage showing through his facial features. So many films came to my mind. Perhaps Al Pacino or another one of the wise guys, or was it *Good Fellows*? I really must brush up on my slang. I didn't know many Northern men well and thought perhaps, yes, maybe only, that I wanted a friendship to develop," Charlotte smiled.

To Travis, it looked like she was coming up for air, and while he looked at a dozing Ramón, he just waited for the next dive in the raconteur-inspired ocean of her memory.

"Looking more closely at him, I noticed a small scar or perhaps a tattoo above his left wrist. Interestingly, it appeared to resemble a flaring "U" or possibly a pair of horns. We continued chatting and getting to know each other until my phone rang. It was my friend Alice calling. She requested that I go up to the desk in the clubhouse to give her a guest pass since she didn't live in the Arbors."

Travis imagined Charlotte rising from her chair and donning her modest cover-up and sparkly flip-flops. She probably left her book and beach bag on her chair, signaling she would come right back and continue their conversation.

"So, I got up, determined to continue where I left off with him, but then I heard a loud shout 'Gino! Hey Gino!' A man was almost running toward us. It was Joe Malinski, and I knew he was a New Yorker. You see, Joe and I have played Bunco and Mexican Train together several times. Sad to say, however, Joe never seemed to be able to get my name right. At times, I have answered to Charlene and Charmaine and rarely corrected him even on the memorable occasion that he called me Lolita. Joe has trouble remembering names, but I have a cousin William who has a similar problem. William taught calculus at the University of North Carolina at Wilmington, so I'm pretty sure that the mental block, if it is one, certainly has nothing to do with intelligence."

"So, you're sure it was Mr. Malinski? And he called Carlo by the wrong name?"

"I sure am. And I looked over my shoulder as Joe called Carlo 'Gino' quite loudly. I briefly assumed they were friends from New York, or Joe was having another of his wrong name episodes."

"And did you see them shake hands or some other form of recognition by Carlo?" Travis asked, gently kicking Ramón's foot to make sure he was paying attention. Ramón sat up straight and coughed lightly.

"No, I didn't. I entered the clubhouse and took the elevator up to the first floor. With these blasted knees, I have to. I remembered the days when I could nimbly leap upstairs two or even three steps at the time. Alice and I took the elevator down, and I told her about Carlo. I was set for her to meet him."

"And?" Ramón interjected.

"It was strange! When we reached the pool, neither Carlo nor Joe Malinski was around anymore. Thankfully, my bag and book were still on my chair."

Chapter 16

First Reconstruction

A low buzz originating from the office's air vents was audible as Travis, Ramón, and Julia were sitting around the table, each looking over their notes. Travis leafed through several pages while Julia checked files on her laptop. Ramón was looking up more information on the murder weapon. After their rather one-sided conversation with Charlotte, the men had hurried back to the station while discussing her biggest revelation about Joe Malinski. Travis closed his notebook and looked up.

"So, with all we have found out, I think we need to start with our victim. Since you checked out the birth certificate, Julia, what have you come up with?"

"We know where he was born, and I did dive into some old records in Scranton. The family Messina lived downtown in the Italian neighborhood and stayed there as far as I could tell from the census records. There are no records of the parents moving to the New York area. That is different from what he told Charlotte about having lived in New York all his life. Of course, we don't know when Carlo moved there, but he doesn't appear in the census records by name. In itself, not an issue, since children's names weren't listed, just the number of children. He could have left after he was eighteen and never established a residence around the Scranton area."

"Good. At least we have uncovered something about Carlo's life in the past century," Ramón commented.

"Oh, but I'm not done," Julia said, tapping on her keyboard. "I checked the school records."

"And?" Travis asked.

"Well, at first nothing. At least not under the name Carlo Messina. In 1968 I did find a Dino Messina in first grade, and I've got to assume that it must be a brother, younger by a year perhaps."

"Didn't they go to the same school?" Travis asked.

"Apparently not. Carlo doesn't appear in any of the Scranton area schools. Just Dino."

"Maybe Dino was his middle name, and he went by that name?"

"There was no middle name on the birth certificate," Julia said. "It's just that the years do not add up. He should have been in second or third grade when Dino pops up in school."

"He could've been held back?" Travis offered, opening his notebook again, underlining Gino's name in the notes he took when talking to Mrs. Beaumont. He wrote Dino on top of it, followed by a question mark.

"I thought so too," Julia said. "Then I went back to the 1970 census and guess what?"

"Well, you said they didn't move, so I'm not sure what you're getting at."

"They listed one son. One! How could that be?"

"An error in dates on the birth certificate?"

"Nope. I found two more things. Ten years later, there was still only one son. But there were two."

"Are you messing with us? Come on, tell us," Travis said. He gently poked Julia in her upper arm with his finger.

"All right," she smiled. "I found a birth record for Dino, the second son."

"You could've told us that right away," Ramón said. "What's the problem?"

"It's obvious," Travis answered before Julia looked up. "The census should've listed two children, and only one was listed. That's what's wrong with this."

"For you to figure out," Julia nodded. "Keep in mind that there are several explanations. Maybe he was sent to live with family somewhere else, perhaps New York or he was institutionalized for some reason."

"True. But somehow, he ended up in the New York area," Travis said. "Any school record there?"

"I already checked that. Nothing in New York or New Jersey."

"There's a small chance that his parents are still alive; a better chance that his brother is," Ramón suggested.

"I figured that too, but no luck. I'll keep searching. I'm using the pictures with some pattern recognition program, which may take days to find a match if it's even possible. The two young kids in the pictures look like brothers, and, as far as I can guess, they're about a year to two years apart. Anyway, what else did the infamous Charlotte tell you?"

"Something interesting," Travis said.

"Hah!" Ramón said, rather loudly. "It took a while before she spilled that interesting thing."

"Oh, what was that?"

Travis stood up. "She told us that Joe Malinski seemed to know Carlo. He called out to him as if he was an old friend."

"Oh, I meant something else," Ramón said. "Remember, she mentioned a tattoo. Was that written up in the coroner's report?"

"Haven't gotten it yet. Not that it matters because I saw the tattoo in the shower. Anyway, let's focus on Joe first."

"And what did Joe tell you when he was in here this morning?" Julia asked.

"He said that he met Carlo inside playing billiards but neglected to mention having seen him at the pool first. It may not be important, but he should have recalled that. It's been less than two weeks," Travis answered and sat down again. He saw Ramón writing something down. "Then again, he admitted he had some issues remembering people. I'm keeping an open mind here."

"Perhaps he's showing the first signs of Alzheimer's or something," Julia offered.

"Be it as it may, he mentioned something interesting that gives him a good amount of credibility," Travis replied.

"The gang?" Ramón asked.

"Exactly. And that's where Charlotte comes in with mentioning a tattoo. Joe mentioned a similar tattoo belonging to a gang named the Torellos. Julia, can you research a gang that ran the streets in New York City about forty or so years ago?"

"I'll be on it," Julia said.

"Thanks. Something else seems confusing. Charlotte confirmed that at the pool, Joe called Carlo by the name Gino. Joe admitted his confusion with people's names and blamed it on the small brain episodes he had. There's not much difference between the names Dino and Gino. I'd understand completely that Joe may have misspoken a few times."

Julia closed her laptop. "Considering that we have the Messina brothers names as Carlo and Dino, Gino isn't that far-fetched. If the census records are any indication, there isn't a third brother. The problem is more that we keep seeing one single son. Something's off."

"What about the birth certificate?" Travis asked.

"It's authentic, signed, and dated the day after birth," Julia answered.

"I get that," Travis said. "so, maybe the census record is wrong. Regardless, the names Dino and Gino are so similar that I think Joe had meant to say Dino. Can you check on whether a Dino Messina ever lived in New York City? Let me know if you find anything."

After Julia left, Ramón checked his notes. "When are you going to see Joe Malinski again?"

"Later today, on my way home. I'm going to check with the Coroner's office first."

"Good luck. It's Sunday, and I'm not sure about staffing. Anyway, I'm going to dig into how Mr. Whitman's card was used to enter the clubhouse last night. I also want to take a closer look at the person in that security camera recording."

Chapter 17

Malinski Elaborates

Travis had sent Julia a copy of the high-resolution picture of Carlo's arm decorated with the dark grey U-shaped logo. It now clearly looked like twin devil tails originating from a round dot, first running sideways for an inch on either side and then straight up. He figured that both Julia and Ramón would stay on to find out all they could about the gang that used this unusual symbol of allegiance.

Driving home, he called Maureen. "Listen, I'm on my way into the neighborhood, but I have about a half-hour stop first. What's for dinner?"

"The salad's ready, and you're barbecuing the chops, remember? They're marinating now."

"Oh, that's right. Great. I'll be there soon," Travis said. He let Maureen hang up the call as he parked his car in front of the Malinski home. He called Joe a bit earlier, giving him a heads up, saying he needed more of his help in the case.

The garden in front of the house was still the same as the ones that the developer had put down years ago. The double knockout roses had shot up pretty high because obviously, they hadn't been trimmed down properly early in the spring. A small fountain wasn't working, and the wood chips looked like last year's. He rang the doorbell and waited.

Joe opened the door. "Come on in, detective."

"Thanks."

"How's the case going since we talked earlier?"

"Oh, we're getting some things lined up," Travis said as they walked toward a sitting area off from the living room. On his left, he noticed a beautiful mahogany upright piano and three comfortable chairs. He estimated that the bookcase running from the floor to the ceiling on his right held more than five hundred books. Joe and or his wife were avid readers, he figured.

"Please sit," Joe said. "Can I get you anything to drink?"

"I'm fine, thanks. Listen, I wanted to follow up a bit on what you told me this morning."

"Sure, as I said, I'm ready to help," Joe said as he sat down.

"You can help me with two things. First, you mentioned that at the suggestion of Marc, you met Carlo in the pool room, but are you sure you didn't meet him earlier, perhaps somewhere else on the property?"

"I thought you wanted my help, detective. I already told you what I remember."

"Rest assured, Joe, your shedding some more light on a few things will help me figure things out. Sort of explaining what I don't understand yet."

Joe stood up and retrieved the drink he was nursing when Travis had come in. Before he sat down again, he briefly slapped his forehead with the palm of his free hand. "Oh, for Christ's sake. I tell you, some things that I think are irrelevant get stored so far away in my brain that I can't recall them when I need to."

"It happens,' Travis said. "And?"

"I don't know why I didn't say anything about it, but yes, I'd seen him a few days earlier, briefly though, at the outside swimming pool. I just said *hello,* and that was it."

"But how did you pick him out at the pool if you didn't know him, and he'd just moved in a few days earlier?"

"You see, it's what I tried to explain to you earlier. The same damn thing happened to me like in the game room. I walked by the outside pool and thought I recognized the man. The name Dino came to mind, and even though I suddenly wasn't sure, I yelled it out to him. He looked up, and I walked over, realizing that I may have made a mistake, wanting to correct it. I decided to wave briefly at him and walked away. How the hell did you find that out anyway?"

"We're never alone, Joe. Another neighbor had witnessed you calling him Gino and saw you walking over to him."

"Yeah, well, for whatever it's worth, I didn't talk to him that day. I thought I said Dino. Anyway, it doesn't matter. We all know it was Carlo."

"I believe you, Joe. I was just wondering why you hadn't mentioned all this, that's all. I do have another question, and believe me: I'm fully aware of the issues you sometimes have with names and remembering people," Travis said and paused.

Joe nodded but remained quiet. He'd been sitting at the edge of his seat the last few minutes, which Travis thought was more of a defensive position. Slowly, Joe sat back a bit and waited for Travis to continue.

"So, all I'm saying is that you may be unaware that you have one of the clues we're looking for." He noticed Joe raising his eyebrows and moved to the edge of his chair again. "You see, I don't think it's at all crazy that you called Carlo by a different name. Maybe you did know him as Gino, or even Dino. We are looking into a discrepancy that pretty much has us confused as well. I'm wondering if you could recall how you knew Carlo. Perhaps the confusion has a basis?"

Joe crossed his legs and looked away for a few seconds as if trying to recall something. "All I know is that he had the same height and build as Gino, with the same big eyes. Still handsome and fit. Now he's dead, and I'm starting to think there's more to the story. You know, when I had my brief talk with him in the clubhouse and realized I wrongly thought he was someone I knew, there was the sudden flash of a nickname, but my brain couldn't catch it. Maybe I'm spinning tales in my head, but could he have turned state's evidence and entered witness protection? Who was he? Do you know?"

Vinder shrugged and reluctantly told him that he, too, was still trying to find that out. He also felt that asking about a tattoo might confuse Joe even more. Perhaps another time. He stood, and Joe did the same. They shook hands. 'Joe, this has been helpful in a way. When this is over, can we get together for a beer or something?"

Joe grinned happily, nodded his assent. "Sounds like a plan, detective. Don't hesitate to call on me. I'd like to help out at any time."

Chapter 18

Julia's Find

Travis hadn't expected a call so late. He checked his phone and couldn't believe Julia was still working at a quarter past nine. He walked over to his small study near the front of the house as he pushed the green button.

"Well, hey there, Julia," he said. "What are you doing so late at the office?"

"Well, you know, with that birth certificate from Scranton in hand, I got to thinking. You see, Travis, the fact that there was just one son with possibly two different names just didn't make sense to me. Something didn't add up. So I went looking for more birth certificates."

"And?"

"Sure enough. I found a second one, but not in Scranton."

"Where and who's?" Travis said, sitting down, feeling that Julia's information may make his night.

"First of all, it was in Wilkes-Barre, just south of there. The names of both parents are on the birth certificate of a Dino Messina in January of 1962."

"So, two children, after all. Proves that those census records are not always correct."

"But they are, that's the find of the night," Julia quickly countered.

Travis said up straight. "How so?"

"Well, it appears that the family had moved for only a short while to Wilkes-Barre, and they were back in Scranton for the next census. What happened before that census was a heartbreaker. You see, I found the death certificate of a young four-year-old named Carlo Messina."

Travis sat back, stunned and at a loss for words.

Chapter 19

Who Is Carlo Messina?

The study room facing the northern side of the house appeared dark, mirroring the outside dusk. Travis had been sitting in this twilight for a while, eyes closed. A few scenarios of how the victim had gotten his name had been filling his thoughts, and he ended up where he began at the start of the day: *Who is this Carlo Messina?*

The information that Julia found relating to a certain Carlo Messina seemed convincing. Still, there was no telling whether there were more people with that name. In any case, there was also the issue of how someone disappeared for almost forty years. He'd never had a situation where that had been part of a person's life story. Could someone disappear from the radar, especially the government radar, for such a long time? He realized that someone who moved overseas for that duration would undoubtedly fall into that category of explanation. Then again, a four-year-old disappearing for many years through childhood and the beginning of adult life seemed very unlikely. He briefly considered the possibility that the young Carlo went to live with relatives. It would explain the census data, but not the death certificate. No. It was clear that regardless of the Messina family situation in the Scranton area, there had been two sons, Carlo and Dino. Carlo was the one who died at a young age. However, the murder victim had his birth certificate and was alive years after that census. Did someone fake the death certificate? Was that the reason Carlo Messina had to move away? An illegitimate child, passed off to relatives far away? He wished there was some info from the brother. That might explain a lot.

Travis got up and briefly stared outside at the street before he closed the blinds. He sat down at his desk and opened his laptop to check his mail's inbox. As expected, Julia had sent him a few emails with links to city records and snapshots of a 1970 individual census record. It was confirmation of what he already knew. Sitting back, he pondered over the meaning of all this. There was one term that came to mind. Maureen had told him once about *ghosting*. He remembered that she was reading a book about someone who had taken another person's name after reading the obituary in the paper. That thief assumed a new identity with the purpose of getting credit cards in the deceased's name. After the credit line on the account dried up, the identity would revert to the original person. Since that was a dead person, the credit card company realized the scam. This criminal ingenuity was something that she found despicable. He had agreed and thought that *ghosting* was the appropriate name. Contemplating the current case and what he'd learned so far, the essence of that type of crime intrigued him.

He turned off his laptop and walked over to the living room. As she did often in the evening after dinner, Maureen was reading a book, most likely a mystery novel, he figured. She looked up over her frameless reading glasses just as Travis was scratching his head, which signaled that he needed to talk about something. She put the book on her lap and took off her glasses.

"Stuck on something?"

"You can say that again. The victim's past is hard to pin down, and I can't figure it out. Remember, a while back we were talking about ghosting?"

"Yeah, I read a book about that. Is that what you ran into?"

"I'm not sure. All I know is that a guy, our victim in this case, pops up with someone else's name. Yet, he may very well be that person."

"Lots of people have the same name, dear," Maureen smiled. "Ghosting isn't what you think it is. More recently, it is more about disappearing from social media somewhere in a relationship."

"Oh? I thought it was about taking someone else's name."

"It may have meant that a while back, but ever since it became a synonym for a thing called ghostwriting, it now evolved into the meaning of the day."

"So what would I call it when someone steals the identity of someone who died a long time ago and runs with it for just the purpose of carrying on his life with that new name?"

"I don't know. Identity theft?"

"Duh, That's too obvious."

"Are you thinking of something else?"

"Of course. I'm sticking with ghosting. You see, if our victim had taken the identity of a child that died a long time ago, it sort of makes that child live on. What's more, if that young person had a social security number, and that too was taken, the new identity would appear to work. The 'ghost' of the young child would live on in the new person, so to speak."

"Do you know for sure that he took the identity?"

"I'm starting to lean that way. First of all, he possessed the birth certificate of a child from Scranton. This means that if it's his valid certificate, he's their son. Secondly, we found it in a woman's wallet. A very old one at that."

"So the guy stole the wallet, and when he found the birth certificate, he might have found out more that worked out when something caused him to take the child's identity."

"If you tend to believe that he's not the true son because Julia did find a death certificate, then that is what happened."

"Well, there you go. You probably solved it, Travis. Glad I could talk you through it," Maureen said and picked up her book again.

Unsatisfied with that conversation, Travis went to the kitchen and filled a glass with cold filtered water from the refrigerator. He took a sip, walked back to his office space, and turned on the light. He checked the time, took out his phone, and made a call.

He spoke rapidly, even before Ramón could manage to say hello, "Ramón, sorry to bother you tonight."

"No problem, Travis," Ramón said. "Got something? What can I do?"

"I've looked at some possibilities regarding the background of the victim. Here's what I'm speculating and hear me out for a second. I believe that Carlo Messina is the name our victim took from the young child with that name on the birth certificate. You should know that Julia told me that this child died young. Somehow, our victim stole the mother's wallet, which we found in the box, and he may have known about the child's passing. I want you and Julia to track down the brother, Dino Messina, as soon as possible. Talk to Julia in the morning.

There may be a small chance that the parents, or one of them, is still alive too."

"We tried that earlier. No luck so far. We also have been looking for other people with that last name in the Scranton area. I think getting even the smallest amount of confirmation from a family member will clear things up."

"Right. And another thing. I was talking with Joe Malinski again. I'm starting to think that he has a point, unwittingly perhaps. What if he did recognize our victim and called him out by his real name?

"Wow, that would be interesting."

"To say the least. But Joe threw another name in the mix, which has me wondering."

"What name?"

"Dino."

"Sounds like Gino. Right. I see that. But there's a real Dino Messina out there. From the pictures of Dino and Carlo, we could see a lot of facial similarities. He may be thinking of him?"

"Not sure until we talk to the real Dino Messina. And then there's another thing. When talking with Kreissman this morning, he too had some vague recollection of having seen our victim before."

"What? This is getting crazy. Where?"

"While the planes hit the trade center in 2001."

"He remembers his rides? I'm starting to think that many Italian characters are looking alike. Remember when Charlotte was rambling on about Pacino and others..."

"So, you were paying attention."

"Of course. I don't miss a thing this woman says. I tend to think she never tells all that she knows, and even now, I feel she's holding back. I always try to anticipate what she's going to spring on us before she even says it."

"Sounds like you want to become an ESP type of detective."

"Ha-ha, funny. You know I want to be just a regular detective."

"I know, back to the case. You realize that if our victim has assumed the identity of the deceased young Messina, we would have to find out who he was before and why he assumed a new name and when. That's going to be hard to figure out."

"Maybe not. I think there's a way," Ramón said.

Travis was surprised at Ramón's remark. Had he overlooked something while a young officer had figured something out? "How's that?"

"I think there's a good possibility that we find a family member of the young Carlo Messina. Running a check on the name that Mr. Malinski has in mind, we can figure it out. After all, how many Gino's are in Joe's old files. Not many, I believe."

"You know, Ramón, you may be right. In the morning, I'll call Joe and Phinn, as I believe both haven't told me all we need to know. We need a little more prodding and a link in New York City."

"I agree, Travis," Ramón said. "Julia and I will be all over that first thing in the morning."

"Keep me informed. I'll be in early."

"We'll see you at the office then. I do have another question, though."

"Shoot."

"What about the murderer? We have the weapon, and we have a decent timeline."

"My take on it, Ramón, is this. If we know who our victim is, we'll be able to determine a motive. That may lead us to the killer. Unless something pops up, we need to take this one step at the time."

"I hear you. See you in the morning."

Travis hung up and grabbed his notebook. He quickly found the number.

Chapter 20

Phinn's Struggle

It was late in the evening, and the events of the day, including his short game of bocce ball, seemed to have happened a long time ago. Mary had already gone to bed, and Phinn was sitting on the couch, trying to figure things out. He was still bothered that he'd lied to the detective, but he'd have to let that go if he was to make sense of what else the murder scene had stirred in him. He hadn't confided any of this to Mary. All she was aware of was that he might be a witness since he and the murdered man were in the same club.

They had retired to North Carolina on a whim and a good deal. It helped, of course, that their son Sean was living in Raleigh. They experienced an abrupt transition to the 55+ active adult community, and what a change! Phinn was used to things happening quickly, people talking fast, people in a hurry, his boss wanting crimes solved yesterday. Even at the security firm, things were happening all the time. But here, life moved at a slower pace, and he had a hard time adjusting. There were over a thousand homes in his new community, all different models and sizes. In the beginning, they all looked alike to him. He kept turning into the wrong driveway until he got his bearings. He wanted to put something big and bright in the front garden to make it unique, but he was afraid of the warning he might receive from the architectural committee. There were many rules, even each bush or tree he wanted to plant had to be authorized ahead of time, and by then, it would be winter, and he had to wait another year. Having been a cop, he was used to rules, laws, but this was a bit much. It seemed to take the retire out of retirement.

He did like the big clubhouse and the fact that there were plenty of clubs, one for just about every interest. Mary was a homebody and loved her books. His chest tightened when he thought of her and how stubborn he'd been after his abduction. It was hard for him to be vulnerable, and he needed all his strength to move forward. She somehow had understood him. She didn't push; she was just there. Thank goodness she was able to care for him without overdoing her part. She understood his need to minimize his trauma on his way to healing. She accepted the alarming pain of PTSD and his loss of ability to think as quickly as he once did.

Unfortunately, within two years of moving to Carolina Arbors, their son was promoted and transferred to Colorado Springs, traveling up the ladder in his company as an IT specialist. Phinn and his son didn't always see eye to eye on things, but Phinn loved him and had a soft spot for his daughter-in-law, Cara. The sensitive loss of safety and contentment of having them nearby left a gaping hole in Phinn's psyche. He realized that he and Mary were here to stay. There was no way he would consider another move. He took another sip from a cold beer and started to think about what he'd seen the night before.

There'd been something familiar about the man lying silently on the floor. He couldn't quite put his finger on it. He'd been getting more forgetful lately, as Mary was quick to point out. In this case, however, that familiarity was strong enough for him to be convincing. It needed to be resolved. He checked the time and decided to give his cousin Patrick a call. Always ready for a cheer-up, and if anyone can help solve the strange familiarity, Patrick would be the one. After all, he'd been a NY medical examiner for a long time and had an excellent memory.

"Hey, Paddy! How's it going?"

"O'Hara! I was just thinking about you the other day and wondering how you were faring down there in the deep south."

Phinn visibly relaxed some at the sound of Patrick's cheerful voice. Oh, how he missed him. "Deep south? Durham?" Phinn retorted back, amused.

"Yeah," said Patrick. "I hear there's a barbecue place on every corner. Barbecue sauce on pizza, spaghetti, you name it." Patrick knew Phinn had a good appetite and was jabbing him to have taken a food quality hit by moving out of New York City.

Phinn said, "Well, I do miss the Ol' Lindenwood Diner in Brooklyn, and how about that Umberto's Clam House in Little Italy. Even though Crazy Joe was shot there in '72, they know how to make the best linguini. Anyway, that's not why I called." Phinn continued. "We had a murder here in our community. Can you believe that?"

"Hey, Phinn, slow down, what's going on? You okay? You sound tense."

"I'm fine, taking a deep breath," Phinn responded and put the phone down for a few seconds. "What I'm calling about is that I saw the victim, and he somehow looked familiar. I figure with your work all these years; you've seen your share of DB's. Maybe he might look familiar to you too? I just can't place him."

"Do you have a picture of the man? If you do, I could run him through our database. You know, you met some pretty scary guys working OCCB. Remember the Lufthansa Airline case at JFK you worked on? They never did recover that $5 million cash, but you still put away some lowlife that was connected. I don't know how you handled it around all the narcotics and gambling. And your surveillance cases with the FBI to uncover mob activities put you around a rough bunch. You inflicted some significant damage to the crime families, and you got lots of perps to testify. But it would sure be weird if some mob connection ends up in your sleepy community. Can you get a picture? If so, send it to me, and I'll check. Mary okay?"

"Yes, she is. Thanks, Paddy. I'll be in touch if I can get the detective on the case here to share a picture."

As Phinn hung up, he realized that he wasn't cheered up as much as he had anticipated. He took a sip of his beer and reminisced about watching the movie *Goodfellas* when it first came out. It was uncomfortably accurate in some respects and reminded him of his cop days in Brooklyn. His mind wandered to the many times he had a cup of coffee and lobster tail pastry with his 75th precinct buddies at the Ferrara Bakery in Little Italy. In rehab, he was encouraged to focus on positive memories. Food was one of them.

The mix of emotional trauma with physical damage caused his life to become a struggle. Phinn couldn't stop his mind from drifting back to when he was abducted outside his home, thrown in a van, and taken as a hostage. The Fortimare Family wanted answers. They wanted names and locations of informants that would testify against one of their own. He didn't remember if he gave up any names, but torture is torture.

His memory loss tormented him, and the guilt ached at his heart. Had he gotten informants killed, or did they make it to witness protection in time? He wasn't privy to that information. But he hoped they got to them in time. He was taken off the case due to his injuries and memory issues and was grateful to have Mary by his side. She was a fantastic caretaker while experiencing one of his lowest moments in rehab. He figured he might not be here if it wasn't for her patience and trust.

He snapped out of his reverie by realizing that he wasn't quite ready to reveal his past struggles against the Mafia to that Detective Vinder. What would Vinder think once he found out Phinn was unfit for duty due to brain trauma? That certainly wouldn't instill much credibility as a witness. Yet he needed to see the detective again if he wanted a picture of that Mr. Messina. Only when he would get any information from Patrick would he then come forward with any theories. But what if the detective began suspecting him of having a grudge due to his trauma, PTSD, and traumatic brain injury? He couldn't bear to be a suspect, and his nerves began to tingle as his cortisol shot up. He needed to make that call tomorrow. He went to the bedroom, hoping for some sleep, which he doubted would come.

Chapter 21

The Real Carlo

On Monday morning, the station was abuzz with the rumor that the victim wasn't who he was supposed to be. Courtesy of Julia, earlier in the morning, a few people had picked up bits of information from her conversation with Ramón in the cafeteria. It didn't take long before Travis heard from others what he already knew. He took his coffee and, on the way to his office, beckoned Julia to follow him.

He pointed at a chair while he remained standing, taking a careful sip of the hot drink. "So, now that everyone seems to know that Carlo may not have been Carlo, what else have you come up with this morning?"

Julia looked surprised. "What are you talking about?"

"Overheard it by the coffee pot."

'Damn. Sorry. We did have a short conversation this morning after I tracked the Messina family."

"Well, that's at least promising. What did you find?"

"We found a Dino Messina who lives outside of Philadelphia. Ramón is probably talking with him now. As for the parents, I haven't found any trace of them yet."

"Where's Ramón?"

"In the second conference room."

"I'll go see him. You keep working on the parents, just in case," Travis said as he left her behind in his office.

Julia relaxed, appreciating that this was about as much as the chewing out she was going to get. She went back to her desk and started searching again.

Ramón held his finger to his lips when Travis entered. He wrote down an email address in his notebook and said goodbye to the other person on the call.

"The brother?"

"Indeed. I think I got the whole scoop on our real Carlo Messina."

"What did Dino tell you?"

"We figured it about right. Dino was the second son of Anna and Al Messina. He confirmed that he was born in 1962. That was two years after his older brother Carlo. The family lived in Wilkes-Barre from 1961 through 1968. In 1964 young Carlo caught the flu, got pneumonia, and unexpectedly died."

"Sad for the family, no doubt," Travis said. "All that explains the numbers we found the census data. What else?"

"Dino told me his mother was inconsolable after little Carlo died. She needed to get away for a while and left to see one of her cousins who lived in Brooklyn. Dino and his dad stayed behind. After a week, they got word that she'd been the victim of a robbery and had ended up in a hospital. The injuries must have been severe because she didn't get home until months later. Both parents passed away a few years ago."

"Did you happen to mention something about a stolen wallet given what he told you about the robbery?"

"I did ask him, and he heard about that much later in life. All he took from that story was that his mother had been sad about losing the money and the pictures."

"And now we have the pictures."

"Should we return them to him?"

"Probably," Travis said and looked at this phone. "Oh, Phinn O'Hara is coming in. Wants to talk to me urgently."

"Really? Interesting," Ramón said as he stood up. "In any case, we need to find out when and why our victim took the little boy's name. I'm not sure that our victim committed the robbery. It's safe to say that somehow he got the wallet and, knowing its contents, realized an option for a new identity. It's possible that once he knew that the real Carlo had died, he was free to use the name when he needed to. What do you think?"

"I spent some time last night going over the possibilities. I agree that, whoever he truly is, he had a particular reason at a certain time to indeed take on the name of the young boy."

"But not knowing his real name, we've got nothing to go on."

"Perhaps. I have a few ideas that may or may not pan out."

"Tell me!"

"Remember, Malinski's confusion with the name when he met our victim at the pool?"

"Yes. So wait, you now believe Malinski? You think he called our victim by his real name?"

"Exactly what I'm thinking. I need to know if it was Dino or Gino. You were going to check into that, by the way?"

"I'm working on it."

"No, have Julia do it. Tell her not to get sidetracked by the robbery almost sixty years ago."

"How's that?"

"Well, obviously our victim couldn't have done it. He was all of four years old at the time. Maybe we'll never find out how he got that wallet, and perhaps that's a question for later. So have Julia check records of criminal cases with the name Gino and perhaps Dino. Preferably between let's say 1980 and 2000. After you tell her, join me when I talk with O'Hara. I'm going to see if he's come in yet. We'll meet in this room."

"Yes. I'd like to join you," Ramón answered. "Regarding Mr. Messina, you should know that I didn't mention that we were dealing with a Carlo Messina here. I just told him we were looking into the Messina name as it related to an old case in New Jersey."

"In our next call, we need to tell him. That may not come until we've solved this case, though."

"I agree."

Travis left the room and headed for the lobby.

Chapter 22

The Mob Hit

Travis noticed right away that O'Hara was in a better state than the day before. Perhaps something that he remembered had enlightened him. He showed him into the interrogation room.

"Oh, this is where you beat the crap out of suspects, huh?" Phinn asked.

"Just any old room," Travis responded, motioning Phinn to sit down. He took out his notebook while he positioned himself across from Phinn. "So, what brings you in today?"

"Well, to tell you the truth, I have done nothing but think about what happened and how I reacted to it."

"And what did you think about?"

"I've been through a lot of stuff in my days, but there's one thing I did well. I brought in the criminals that others didn't find. I made sure they faced justice. I caught not only the petty crime jerks but also the big guys, the bosses, and their lieutenants. It didn't matter to me. Once I knew for sure what they'd done, I brought them to the detectives."

"Is that what you're doing now?"

"This one is different. I ain't no longer a cop, you see. But that doesn't mean I don't know how to recognize what has transpired here."

"So, if you were still a cop, what would you tell me since I'm the detective?"

"I'd tell you who's done the slashing and why."

Travis was intrigued. Here was a man who right out the gate had lied to him, yet now it seemed that the whole reason he went into that bathroom was to ascertain what happened, based on his experience. Travis decided not to bring that up negatively, but as he sat up, he couldn't resist. "So, you had an inkling all along that something was wrong in that bathroom, and you needed to see it for yourself to put your experience to work?"

"Something like that. Of course, I didn't know what I would run into, but I was curious enough to check it out. It brought out so many emotions in me, so much that I couldn't handle it, detective. You know very well that this wasn't the first DB I'd seen. I know a thing or two about crime scenes and what they're telling me. Now, I know you have most likely seen your share too, but this one stood out."

"And when did you realize that?"

"Probably immediately. Not that I dealt with it. As I said, there was plenty of trauma for me in my last case. It's one I couldn't help solve because I never went back on the beat. So forgive me for taking some time, but I think you should know that what I saw may help your case."

Travis sat back again. Phinn O'Hara was taking his time. It looked more like he was laying the foundation of the case he was about to make. Travis hadn't taken any notes yet but felt that this was about to change. "We can always use the help, Mr. O'Hara," he said. "I'm listening."

"This was a mob hit. Period. No doubt about it."

"And why would you say that?"

"It was the execution-style used: making sure there was no sound, so guns were out, and then there's the way a pro slashes the throat. No amateur could've done that. A clean, one single cut slash without any hesitation. Mob style. I've seen many of them. I just didn't know the mob was here in North Carolina." Phinn paused, sitting on the edge of the chair, anticipating some immediate response from the detective.

Travis stood up and paced between the table and the door, back and forth. He nodded a few times and finally stopped, resting his hands on the table. "Well, you may be right about that. I'm picking up the medical examiner's report in a little while, and I wouldn't be surprised to learn that same fact. It was a perfect deadly cut." He paused, and there was a knock on the door. Ramón walked in and sat down on the other chair facing Phinn. "Officer Acosta is joining since he's working the case with me."

"Oh, okay. Good," Phinn said, nodding briefly towards Ramón. He continued the moment he looked back at Travis. "But the examiner can't tell you who did it. I mean the type of person who did it."

"Most likely not. Then again," Travis said, sitting down again, "You don't know who did either. Am I right?"

"I don't have a name if that's what you're asking. But I've seen this crime scene before, as I told you. It was a mob hit by a young killer, quick and precise. I've seen it, and the scene looked the same."

"How so?" Travis asked.

"First of all, the shower. You see, killing someone that way causes a gush of blood with a lot of splatter. It's all over the floor, the walls, on the body, but also the killer. Invariably when the body drops, blood squirts everywhere, and the killer gets his share."

"I see. So you think that is what happened here?"

"I'm sure of it. Also, I'm sure that nobody in the building saw a man walk out with blood on his shirt, jacket and pants, right?"

"Not that we know of," Travis responded. He felt he was getting a lesson in the immediate aftermath of a murder. He'd been through his own experience and training a long time ago, but nobody had ever described it the way Phinn was doing. "We checked the security videos and nothing has popped up."

"And you won't find such a person either. No, I have a pretty good idea of what happened."

"You can tell all that from having seen the body for just a few seconds?" Ramón asked.

"Detective," Phinn responded, straightening the collar of his polo shirt a bit. "What I saw was important, of course, but it took me a full day to recuperate from that. It was during that time that things came back to me, and the more I thought about it, the more I started to figure it out."

"So, what did you think happened?" Travis asked.

"The killer hid in the shower area and waited until Carlo showed up. Now, to make it seem like he wasn't intruding when other people came into the room, he had to dress the part. I figure he had a bathing suit on, looking like he just got out of the shower, drying himself off, meanwhile scouting the room. So even if anyone from our men's club had entered, nobody would've thought it strange. He may have used a disguise of some sort to look a bit more our age here in the community.

Most people don't size up a person that closely, and frankly, they went there to relieve themselves and head back to the dinner."

"So you think the killer wore swimming trunks?"

"Could very well be. Anyway, once Carlo came in, all the killer had to do was make sure they were alone. After that, it took less than fifteen seconds to approach, slash the throat, drag the body to the shower, and close the curtain. He would've turned on the shower and use a wet towel to wipe up the floor and then the walls quickly. More than likely, he took a shower with the body lying below his feet, cleaning himself of any evidence. All that would be left was to dry himself off. I bet he left the shower running when he left, washing away any remaining blood."

Travis and Ramón were sitting down, a bit stunned and spellbound by Phinn's story. Of course, it seemed plausible, but it would've sounded a little more like fantasy any other day. How many cases like this could there have been? And how did he know? Travis rubbed his eyes. "So, you're telling me that it was a hit job by a younger man, made to look older, dressed in swimming gear? Someone, who chose the location on purpose given the facilities at the clubhouse, and then calmly walked out?"

"That about sums it up."

Travis took a deep breath and looked at Ramón, who simply raised his shoulders and slightly shook his head. "Okay, let's go with this for now. Why Carlo? He had a good job before he retired and moved to the Arbors. From what we know so far, it doesn't appear that he had any mob ties. In that case, a hit job would not seem plausible."

"Oh, but that's where I think I can be of some help," Phinn responded. "You see, I have a funny feeling that Carlo isn't really Carlo."

Travis couldn't hide his surprise. How did this man reach the same conclusion he had, but only after some determined detective work? He felt like he was given a lesson here in sleuthing. Was it a bit of revenge for making the man confess to a lie yesterday? No, that couldn't be it. Nevertheless, the man across from them seemed to be a man comfortable with his analysis of the crime, and with a demeanor that confirmed his substantial expertise as a tough New York cop. "Who is he then?" he asked.

"Well, that I'm not sure of, but I know someone who can help us find that out."

Ramón sat up too, having taken out his small notebook, ready to jot down a name. "Who," he asked before Travis had a chance.

"My cousin Patrick, the one I mentioned yesterday."

"A medical examiner in the City, right?" Travis remembered.

"Yep. I talked with Patrick because I have a hunch, you see."

"About what?"

"About the man that called himself Carlo. Now, don't go thinking I see ghosts or anything, but when I saw Carlo the first time before the dinner, he reminded me of some punk I tried to put away a few times. At one point, he worked for the mob, killed a cop, and killed one of the Fortimare lieutenants if I remember correctly. It seemed like both the good and the bad guys wanted him. But it's been over twenty-five years, and I'd forgotten about him, even his name. For all I knew, he somehow ended up in the witness protection program or perhaps in jail. I don't know. One thing I'm sure of is that if he's the one I'm thinking about and the mob found him, that's one of the ways they would've killed him."

"And do you have a name?" Travis asked.

"That's where my memory fails me. But don't worry. All you need to do is send a picture to my cousin; he'll run it through the database. Facial recognition is pretty fast these days."

"You mean, your cousin could give us a name?"

"If the guy's on the computer, you will get a name. I swear. Here is Patrick's number," Phinn said, sliding a handwritten note to Travis.

"But, you've got absolutely no idea?" Ramón asked.

Phinn took a sip of water and stared at the ceiling for a while, finally resting his gaze upon Ramón. "If I had to guess, only a first name comes to mind."

"And that is..." Travis said.

Phinn sat back and mulled it over for a bit, perhaps indicating some uncertainty. He looked at both Travis and Ramón.

"Joe."

Chapter 23

Fingerprints

After Phinn O'Hara left, four people stood around Vinder's desk. Julia had a tablet in her hand, using her stylus as she took notes. Ramón checked his little notebook while the captain was on his phone. They'd all gathered to give him an update on the case. Stephan, the head of forensics and wearing a white coat, spread the report pages for all to see.

"As we expected, the coroner's report confirms a deep, oblique, long incised injury on the front of the neck. There were no hesitant or defensive injuries. The cause of death was a cut throat. It says here that these findings were compatible with a lethal slit throat executed by a right-handed person from behind with the victim's head firmly restrained."

"And did you guys check for prints on the knife?"

"We did after we confirmed that this particular hunting knife was used to murder Mr. Messina. We found it was wiped clean."

"How about prints on the door handles and surfaces in the downstairs room?" Travis asked.

"Nothing inside, and that includes the door handle of the door leading to the Carolina Room and all faucets and shower knobs. However," Stephan answered and paused to check something. "We did find some clear prints on the outside door towards the pool."

"And did you match them with anyone?"

"We just did. A person who lives at the Carolina Arbors."

"What? Someone from that neighborhood is in your database?" the Captain asked. "Who was it?"

"A man named James Whitman."

"Are you kidding me?" Travis asked, jumping up. "How did he ever get into your database? The man has been bedridden after a stroke for the past two months."

"Well, to your second point, I have no clue how that can be the case because those were pretty good prints. As to the man being in the database, that's easily explained. About twelve years ago, he appeared to be part of an insurance fraud ring. According to the findings, he ended up just being in the wrong place at the wrong time. Whatever that meant. I'm not familiar with the case, but that's how his prints came up."

"Perhaps you guys need to pay another visit to the home of Mr. Whitman," the captain said. "Something's not kosher there."

"You're right about that," Travis admitted. "As a matter of fact, when we went there, we never saw Mr. Whitman, only his wife. We didn't bother insisting, having gotten the story from the staff at Piedmont Hall that they hadn't seen him for months. The members of the men's club told me he had resigned because of illness."

"I'll check into that insurance fraud case," Julia offered and left the room.

"Anything else for me?" Stephan asked.

"Not at this time," Travis answered. "Thanks for bringing in the report."

Both the captain and Stephan left.

"What the hell are we dealing with here?" Travis asked, not expecting an immediate answer from Ramón.

Ramón nodded and reflected for a few seconds. "We need to go over and see that Mr. Whitman, but first, what did you think of Mr. O'Hara's story?"

"I have no clue where he got all that. It was as if he was there, watching the crime unfold. It seemed unreal but realistic at the same time."

"Too bad, he didn't see Mr. Whitman in the locker room."

"Yeah, right," Travis smiled. "You're funny."

"It was an incredible analysis of what may have transpired."

"And it pointed directly at a person who was ready to take a shower, most likely just wearing trunks, with a towel ready."

"Amazing. Not only do we have Mr. Whitman on camera entering the men's locker room from the outside, but we also have found his fingerprints. We also know he left two hours later."

"He may have gone to the upstairs locker room and put his towel in the spinner to get most of the water out."

"We've got the video of him leaving," Ramón said. "Do you want to see it again?"

"In a minute. First, we've got another part of the puzzle to contemplate."

"I think I know where you're going," Ramón said. "The name that O'Hara mentioned, right?"

"I was almost sure he was going to say Gino, but then it was suddenly he said the name Joe. What the hell is going on? Are we dealing with two older men who seem to recall our victim by different names? This name confusion is getting crazy."

"At least we know for sure that Carlo wasn't the real name of the victim."

"True. Did you send that picture to O'Hara's cousin in New York?"

"I did. Haven't heard anything back yet."

"Right. Well, let's head over to the Arbors again, and this time we're going to see Mr. Whitman."

Chapter 24

Mr. Whitman

Mary Whitman was surprised to see both Travis and Ramón again. "Oh, no, what is it this time?" she said, stepping outside and closing the door behind her.

"We wonder if we could have a word with your husband regarding that incident we talked to you about before?" Travis said.

"Shh," she said. "I don't want to upset Jim again. I told him why you were here earlier, and he's gotten all worried, saying he has nothing to do with any of this. I suggest you leave unless you have some good reason to get him all upset."

"I understand," Travis said. "Given his situation, it isn't easy to be called on by the police..."

"Especially when he has nothing do with anything at the clubhouse."

Ramón stepped back a bit to look through the front window when he thought he heard someone inside. It was just a hunch, but nothing was revealed given the limited view through the partly opened blinds.

Travis figured he'd give it another try. "Now, I gathered from people at the clubhouse that your husband was an avid swimmer."

"That he was," Mary answered. "Fifty laps a day, every single day. He was especially fond of doing that in the outside pool. He never trusted the inside pool to be clean and germ-free."

"And given his condition, he hasn't been able to get out, which may be upsetting as well."

"Yes, he misses it a lot," she said.

"Now, when he went swimming, did he indeed just go out in his swimming trunks and towel?"

"Oh, yes. And in flip-flops. That's Jim's trademark."

"And, if I may ask, where is his towel now?"

"In the laundry room. Why do you ask?"

"Just making sure it hasn't been used recently."

"Now that's funny. It was in its usual place on the shelf next to the dryer. It was damp for some reason. It was odd, but I just put it in the dryer, and it's back there all folded up. Is there something with the towel?"

"We have some idea why that towel was damp, Mrs. Whitman," Travis answered. "That's why we're here. You see, we have a video of a man carrying a similar towel."

"Where?"

"In the clubhouse, the evening of the murder."

"But that's impossible, detective. Neither my husband nor I was there that night."

"Do you leave the house often, ma'am?" Ramón asked.

"Of course. Mostly in the morning to the yoga class and the grocery store. Why?"

"And who takes care of your husband while you're out?"

"Nobody. At least not on the days a nurse comes in to bathe him. Our insurance covers the service for five days a week."

"And you go out while the nurse is here?"

"Yes, I do take that opportunity."

"I understand," Travis said. "Now, let me tell you. Your husband is in no kind of trouble, and I would like to talk to him. I believe that he can help us."

Mary crossed her arms. "You will just upset him."

"Not if I tell him what his buddies Joe, Mike, and Phinn have told me."

"Oh, those guys. Yes, they're good guys. He was so sorry having to leave that club."

"They wish him the best, but I would like to tell him a little about how they've been helping us out."

Mary thought about it for a few moments, turned around, and opened the door. "All right, come on in, but please wait here until I get him ready."

Travis and Ramón waited by the front door as Mary disappeared into the ground floor master bedroom. They heard her talking and moving chairs around. It took another few minutes before the door opened, and she beckoned them in.

Jim Whitman was sitting up in his bed, leaning against two big pink pillows, his hair neatly combed. Although pale looking, he seemed strong enough to raise his hand as a greeting. He tucked the neatly folded white sheets closer to his waist. Two chairs were at an angle on his side of the bed, facing him. Mary straightened out his pajama top collar and motioned for the men to take a seat.

"Hi, Jim," Travis started. "Thanks for seeing us for a few moments." He noticed that Jim looked a lot skinnier than in the video. Still, then again, the quality of that recording wasn't excellent.

Jim coughed and then swallowed hard. "No problem, detective," he said with some difficulty as there was minimal movement on the left side of his mouth. He labored on, "So how are my pals from the club?"

"Oh, all three are fine, and they helped us a bit with our current case. Joe and Phinn were on the police force in New York, so they had some stories to tell. Mike gave us some insights into his life in the city, but you probably know all that."

"Yes, I do," Jim said. "But what case?"

Travis looked briefly at Mary, making sure she didn't object to telling Jim about it. "Simply put, it's a murder case. Someone was killed in the downstairs men's locker room Saturday night."

Jim's eyes grew wide, and strangely enough, he produced a bit of a smile. "No wonder Phinn and Joe are helping out. Small stuff for those guys." The word guys sounded more like gays, but Jim was working hard to make himself understood.

"We have no suspect or a name, but we have a security video that shows someone who looks like you going into that room."

Jim propped himself up straighter using his fists. "Hah! Now you know that's not possible. I can hardly walk, detective."

"That's what we figure too. But listen to this. The man had a white baseball cap on, a pair of dark blue swimming trunks, a pink towel over his shoulder, and he wore pink flip-flops..."

Jim looked at Mary. "Somebody copied my trademark outfit!"

"Yes, that's what it sounds like, dear," Mary said.

"So, we're looking for somebody who wanted to look like you," Travis said.

"Yes, somebody who used your signature outfit," Ramón added.

"We haven't given his clothes to anyone if you think we had anything to do with this. Not many people come here," Mary said.

"I believe you," Travis said. He wanted to get to the one thing that she mentioned earlier. "Now, the only person who does come here often lately is a nurse. What's her name?"

"Not her, him!" Jim said.

"Oh, I'm sorry about that," Travis said. "A male nurse. Well, what's his name, and who does he work for?"

"His name is Jerry," Mary answered for Jim, who had slid down a little more under the covers. He nodded. "Jerry Darcay, pronounced Dar-say but spelled with a *c*," she clarified.

"And the service company?"

"He came recommended."

"Who recommended him?"

"An old buddy of mine in New York," Jim said.

"I see. How did that person know of your situation?"

"Mary called Roger after it happened."

"Roger?"

"We called him Roger, but his name is Ruggeri."

"Got it," Travis said. "So, do you have any idea where Jerry lives?"

"I think he once said he had a place somewhere on Highway 70 in Durham. I'm not sure where exactly."

"So, you pay him a check weekly?"

"Oh, no," Mrs. Whitman said. "We pay cash."

Travis jotted down the information and looked up. "Your insurance doesn't pay his company directly?"

"No. We get the money from the insurance company," Mary clarified."

"I see," Travis said. "And when is Jerry coming back?"

"He'll be here tomorrow morning, first thing. He had the weekend off, and yesterday he called to say he had an emergency today."

"Thanks. I guess that'll do it."

"Say hello to my pals, okay?" Jim asked.

"Yes, I will," Travis said. "If we need anything else, we'll check with Mary. I trust you'll get better."

Jim waved the men on, and they walked out of the bedroom. Once the door was closed, Travis continued with his questions.

"So, would you happen to have a number for Jerry?"

"I sure do, detective," Mary said. "Just a minute."

Mary went to a small room set up as a home office and returned with a business card. "This is his. I reckon it's just his name and mobile phone number. What do you want to know from him?"

"The usual, a bit of a background check," Travis smiled. "Nothing to worry about."

"Oh, but he's such a nice man. He's a lot stronger than he looks. He has no problem lifting Jim right out of bed."

"How old is he?"

"Not sure. Around forty, I think. It has never come up."

"Okay. Well, thanks," Travis said. "I think we have all we need."

As Ramón and Travis walked toward the front door, Travis turned around. "Oh, one more thing. Did you ever find that access card to the clubhouse?"

"As a matter of fact, I did. It was in Jim's swimming trunks. I was going through some clothes to reorganize, and there it was. He must have left it there the last time he went swimming before his stroke."

"Do you mind getting the card?"

"Not at all, give me a minute."

Ramón stood still by the door. "Is it possible that those trunks were damp as well?"

"Oh, that was my next question," Travis answered.

Mary just walked in before Travis finished his sentence. "You sure have a lot of questions, detective. What else do you need to know?"

"I couldn't help wondering whether, just as that towel, were the swimming shorts damp as well?"

Mary had a puzzled look on her face. "No, why would they be?"

"Just checking. Thanks for your help," Travis said as he took the access card using a tissue he fished from his pocket. He put it in a small evidence bag that Ramón held out for him.

Chapter 25

The Good And The Bad

Standing outside the Whitman's home, Travis called the number on the card. There was no answer.

"Finding this Jerry guy, assuming he's our suspect killer, will be challenging, I'm afraid."

"Why? All we need to do is be here early tomorrow morning, and he will walk in our arms."

"I wouldn't count on that, Ramón. If Jerry's our guy, I bet you he will be a no-show. When we go on what Phinn told us, he's a hitman who finished his job. No reason to hang around. He's long gone."

"And his phone?"

"A burn phone, most likely."

"What's our next step?"

"The clubhouse again. We need to take a better look at that video. I noticed that Mr. Whitman has a slight hunch, and his head skews a bit to the left. Let's see if we see that in the picture."

"I'll let them know we're on our way."

Both men drove off in their vehicle toward Piedmont Hall.

Paulina was already sitting at the security PC in the back office when Travis and Ramón walked in. She had queued the video to the moment Mr. Whitman walked through the foyer.

"Is there any way we can get a picture of this and improve it?" Travis asked.

"I can try," Paulina answered. She hit a few keys and pasted a single picture into a graphics application. A few more clicks later, and a sharper image emerged. "Is this what you're looking for, detective?"

"Yes, thanks. Can you zoom in on it a bit?"

The larger picture showed someone looking like Mr. Whitman, but there was no listing of the head to the left. Ramón was about to say something, but Paulina beat him to it. "Wait a minute," she said. "This is odd. This man isn't Mr. Whitman at all! I mean, the hat, the towel, and the trunks all fit, but this guy has a bit more flesh on the bones. Also, his forehead seems smaller. If I had to guess, this is Mr. Whitman twenty-five years ago!"

Travis nodded. "Right you are, Paulina. We are looking at an imposter here who's whole demeanor is a bit off from the man we just visited."

"And we know who it is," Ramón volunteered.

"Who is it?" Paulina asked.

"Well, let's say that we have a name at this point," Travis butted in. "That's all. Perhaps you can spend some time today with Ramón looking through some videos taken two or three days before the murder?"

"I'm afraid I have too many other things to do," Paulina said, looking at her watch. "I actually should be back at the front desk right now. You can check with the manager, and perhaps he can give you guys the tapes."

Paulina went to the manager's office while Ramón and Travis walked to the foyer. Standing by the windows, Ramón spoke first.

"So if this Jerry character is our man indeed, how did Mr. Whitman's fingerprints get on the door handle?"

"The murderer planted them. All he had to do was lift the prints from a glass in the house. The night of the murder, he transferred them on the handle."

"How?"

"We need to check with Stephan, but I bet that after he brushed a light powder on the glass, he lifted the print with regular tape. He then pressed the piece of tape on the door handle. Check with forensics to see if they detected any sticky residue on the door handle. That would be a dead give-away."

"I will, as soon as I have those tapes. I'll be heading to the precinct right away."

"Good. I'm heading out. I need to call Phinn's cousin. Let me know right away what Stephan tells you and if you see our suspect on another security video."

Ramón walked back to the front desk to check on Paulina. Travis headed for his car.

As he drove on 70 Business into Durham, Travis got the call he was anticipating. The area code was 212. "Travis Vinder," he answered.

"Hello, Detective Vinder, this is Patrick O'Grady."

"Yes, thanks for calling back. I'm sure you guys are always busy in the City."

"We are. Listen, I've talked with Phinn, as you know, and I got the picture your assistant sent me. I have good news and bad news. The good news is that we can help you in your case because we've identified your victim."

"That's great news, Patrick," Travis said, slowing down just in time before running a light. "What's his name?"

"His name is Gino Barese."

"Gino? That's incredible," Travis said. "Any info on him?"

"How about a file about 4 inches thick!"

"The guy was known to the authorities, I guess," Travis said. "Any way I can get my hands on that?"

"I don't have access to that, but I know somebody with whom you'll need to speak. I'll send you all we have here at our office via email."

"So, what's the bad news?"

"Gino Barese died almost twenty years ago."

Travis pulled into the precinct parking lot and stopped. "What? Did you identify a dead man twice? How's that possible? I'm confused."

"Are you sitting down for this one?" Patrick asked.

"Just pulled into the parking lot. I'm sitting in my car. What are you telling me?"

"Truthfully, we've identified him only once. We didn't see his body the first time. Now, there's an explanation for that, but I'm not sure you'll be happy to hear it."

"I have a feeling I won't, but let's have it."

"Gino Barese died in the World Trade Center on September 11, 2001."

Travis, leaning hard into the head-rest, saw Ramón pull up in the lot and rush to the entrance. He tried to conjure up some quick explanation of what he just heard but failed. "Wait, he died in the towers? Was anything proven? I mean, we all heard how difficult it was to find remains."

"I've already checked for you, and two vital facts point in that direction. First, Gino had an appointment with an insurance company at nine that morning on the South Tower's 54th floor. The meeting appeared in a digital appointment book on a database stored off-site. The plane hit the tower two minutes after nine. If one didn't make it out in time, the building collapsed one minute to ten. Second, his neighbors reported him missing within days of the collapse, and they never saw him again. His place looked like he expected to return."

Travis took a deep breath. "Yet, Gino Barese lies in a morgue in Raleigh, a few days after he was very much alive. Are you sure we're talking about the same Gino Barese?"

"The one and only. We are sure of that. When you see the file, you'll know for yourself."

"Then he didn't die at the World Trade Center. He somehow got out in time, ditched everything he ever had, or belonged to, and took on a new identity," Travis concluded.

"That's what I figure, and I'm sure you weren't going to be happy with this piece of information."

Travis got out of the car and walked toward the building. "I tell you, Patrick. This turn of events explains quite a bit. Let me get to my desk and call you back. Is that okay?"

"Sure, I'll be here. Take a look at what I just emailed you before you call me."

"Will do," Travis said, scratching his head as he pushed open the door to his office.

Chapter 26

Identities

Ramón was using Travis' office to view the video he'd collected from the clubhouse. He concentrated only on the recorded images of the outside near the entrance to the downstairs locker room. The search was easy because Paulina found the time Mr. Whitman's access card was used three days before the murder. As he suspected, he saw a man in a white cap open the door. This time the suspect wore blue jeans and a green polo. He was the same height as Mr. Whitman and appeared wary of the camera to his side, at one point shielding his face with his hand. Ramón ran the video for a few more minutes, and as he expected, the man came out again. For about two seconds, his full-face turned toward the camera enough to do a screen capture. "Gotcha," Ramón said to himself. He saved the image in a graphic file. He was about to send a copy to Travis when the detective walked in.

"We've got him," he said jubilantly, pointing at the picture on the screen.

"And we got our victim's real name too," Travis said. "We've got our work cut out."

Ramón didn't know where to start. "What's his name, and how is he connected to our suspect?"

"Our dead man's name is Gino Barese. I should have part of his file in an email. I think that as soon as we know everything about Gino, our suspect will connect somewhere along the way. I hope."

"I'm guessing that our suspect's name isn't Jerry. What do you think?"

"I agree. This whole alias name usage stems from wanting to hide real identities. Partly to throw us off, but also to cover up something. As I said, Ramón, we've got work to do. Let me check my email first. Go ahead and print out a picture of the suspect. Call the Whitmans to find out what kind of car Jerry drives and then set up an APB. If he's still in the state, we could get lucky."

"Good idea. But tell me first, how did you find out the name of the murder victim?"

"That picture you sent on to Phinn's cousin in Manhattan proved to be a winner. We're dealing with a changed identity after 9/11. I'll explain later. Go and get that APB out."

"Sure. I'll be back soon," Ramón said, shutting down the video.

Travis opened his email from Patrick. The attachment was five pages of background on Mr. Barese. Although no DNA evidence was available, a select committee on 9/11 concluded that Mr. Barese was deemed to have perished in the World Trade Center's attack. The specific info on Gino Barese mentioned that he was a low-level criminal tied to the mob. He also had been an informant to the NYPD. He was a suspect in various crimes, most noticeable the murders of a police officer and a mobster.

Travis reflected on the information as he read on. No wonder, he figured, Mr. Barese was interested in changing his identity and in letting his former self disappear in a cloud of dust. It was evident that the background information only dealt with what was known about him for a few years before his first declared death. What was he like before that, and what did he do?

Ramón walked back in. "All set with the APB. The Whitmans said it was a black Honda Civic. They never looked at his license tag. Also, his phone is still off."

"Very well. I'm not sure the APB will help us, but if we assume he's a hired killer like Phinn said, he's skipped town by now. Have a few officers check all the motels along Highway 70 from the airport to Durham. Also, they need to check with the car rental agencies to see whether Jerry fits the description of a man renting that type of car."

"That's all fine, Travis. There's something I don't understand. Why has he been here for months? I mean, Carlo, sorry, uh, Gino, only moved here a few weeks ago. It's as if the killer knew he was moving to that particular neighborhood."

"It has crossed my mind. Jerry, or whoever he is, established a pretty good cover, which begs the question, who is the guy who recommended him? There must be a connection between the Whitmans, the guy they called Roger, and our suspect. Care to do some digging into this yourself?"

"Thanks, I'd be happy to," Ramón smiled. "Tell me, what's up with the Barese name?"

Travis quickly brought the young officer up to date and saw Ramón shaking his head. "What are you thinking, Ramón?"

"It's such a dishonor to the other victims of 9/11. He benefitted from a calamity as he was one of the few that escaped from the building. I wonder how he pulled that off."

Travis thought about it for a few seconds. "Well, come to think of it, this meshes a bit with what Mike told us. Remember the ride that day he gave to a stranger?"

"That would be just too much of a coincidence. No way. Are you planning to talk to him again soon?"

"I hadn't scheduled it. Even if that's what happened, it doesn't further our investigation. Anyway, we'll see."

"I understand. So, how are you going to find out more about Barese?"

"I'm calling Patrick again in a few minutes and see what else we can get. I don't think they're going to send me a thousand or so pages of Barese's case file."

"Looks to me like you're going to take a trip."

"Perhaps. Anyway, keep me informed about what you and other officers find regarding Jerry, and maybe we'll happen upon his real name. That would help us to find out how our victim and killer are connected."

"Okay," Ramón said and left the office.

Travis checked his calendar for the next few days while he dialed. "Patrick, it's me again. Thanks for sending that information."

"No problem, detective. I trust it was useful."

"It's a start, honestly. I can also share with you how your so-called bad news matches what we had found so far."

"I'm listening."

"The man you identified as Gino Barese was known here as Carlo Messina. We ran into a problem because at first, we couldn't find any record of him before 2002. Now we know why. He didn't take the new name until after 9/11. We also found out where he got that new identity. He took the name of a child that died very young in the early sixties, pretty much matching his age. He stayed under the radar for a long time. Somehow by moving to North Carolina, he may have exposed his true identity. I further believe someone hired a hitman to eliminate him. If that happened for what he was, or what he did over twenty years ago, we don't know. We've got to sort out a lot of things."

"With what you said, I believe you have your guy. You did read that he was in trouble with both the mob and the law, right?"

"I did, but I'd prefer to think that the mob would be the one sending out a hitman. Anyway, I believe we have a picture of the suspected murderer. Can we send that to you as well? Our database hasn't turned anyone up so far."

"Sure, I'll have it run through the process, who knows what will turn up."

"Thanks. Concerning Mr. Barese, how can I get access to his file?"

"I just know there is that extensive file. You'd have to contact someone who either was on the case before or someone who can let you look at it. I believe it's probably best you come to the City. I'll call you later."

"That's fine. And I'm sending that picture to you now."

Travis hung up, scanned the APB, and forwarded it to Patrick. As he was making notes about calling both O'Hara and Kreissman, Ramón walked back in.

"What? Did I miss your conversation with the medical examiner? What else did he say?"

"He didn't add anything to the case. We now know about as much as he does. I did send him the APB. He's going to run the guy through the system. What did you find out?"

"The officers are still canvassing the hotels and motels. I decided to call the rental agencies, and I struck gold with

Budget. The desk manager remembered a fellow from my description of Jerry. Our suspect returned a black Honda Civic yesterday morning."

"Did you gather credit card info?"

"Yes. It was in Jerry's name. He had pre-paid for three months but only used two."

"The bird has flown. How about a driver's license?"

"Yes. The manager is sending me a copy. It was issued four years ago in New York City to Jerry Darcay."

"So, that at least matches, but unless they verified it, I'd consider it fake. For that matter, the credit card may belong to a fake identity as well."

"I'll track it with our colleagues in New York."

"Good. You stay on the suspect until you find out his real name. If I hear from Patrick when there's a result from their face recognition system, I'll let you know."

"We'll find him. Don't worry. How are you getting access to Gino's case file?"

"It's like you said earlier. I'm going to take a trip. If I can get on a flight tomorrow morning, I'm out of here."

"I'll stay in touch."

"Of course. Don't forget to check out that guy, Roger. You may need to contact the Whitmans again. Once I'm in the City, I'll decide if I need to see him."

"Gotcha," Ramón said and left.

Travis made another call and hurried home.

Chapter 27

Tying Up Loose Ends

Mike Kreissman and his wife had an early dinner, and Vinder apologized for interrupting with his call. He told them he'd call later because he needed to follow up on their previous conversation.

He arrived at his house and told Maureen about his flight to the City the next morning. She wasn't surprised. "With all those New York connections in that quartet, I was wondering how long it would take for you to trace things back to that area."

"I'd rather do it from here," he said, grabbing a small carry-on suitcase from under their bed. "I left Ramón in charge of a few things. He's digging into more information on our murder suspect while I'm looking for a motive. The victim's past holds a clue, I'm sure."

"Can't they just send you that file?"

"It's over a thousand pages, and everything is either handwritten or typed. I'm still trying to find out who I need to see and where exactly I need to go."

"So, the three other members of that group are off the hook?"

"I know one of them is," he said, opening drawers and stuffing clothing into the suitcase. "I'm giving him another quick call before we have dinner. I also need to get in touch with that ex-detective in that group. I don't think he's told me everything."

"Do you believe he knew the victim under that old name?"

"Maybe. I'll find out."

Travis was all packed and checked his email for a message from Julia. She booked him on the earliest flight on United Airlines. He saw a departure at 6:30 AM. Not ideal, but that would put him in the city by 9:30 at the latest. He planned on two full days with a late return the second day. He checked in on-line and called Mike.

"Detective, sorry about that call earlier," Mike said. "I wasn't sure how long our conversation would be."

"I understand. Sorry for the interruption. I wanted to briefly talk to you about the man you mentioned picking up at the World Trade Center on 9/11. I'm sure it will be hard to recall, but do you remember what time you left the area with that man?"

"I'm guessing it was a bit after nine. I'm not sure. Maybe ten after. I dropped my first ride off at quarter to nine. That I remember. I didn't stay for longer than half an hour, tops. It took a while to help all those people cross the street toward the church. So, yeah, at most ten after."

"That's a pretty good recollection, Mike," Travis said. "There's nothing wrong with your memory."

"Well, thanks. Was that important?"

"Well, you confirmed two things for us. You got the time frame right. I wouldn't doubt that since just about everyone knew where they were when the attack on the towers occurred. Also, your vague recollection of Carlo was spot-on."

"Good. Glad to have been of help. By the way, do you know if there's going to be a service here for the man?"

"That's something I don't know. I'll be talking to a few people in New York tomorrow, and I feel there may be some kin there. I'll let you guys know when I find something out."

"Thanks," Mike said and hung up.

It wasn't until about an hour later when Travis called Joe Malinski. "Joe, how are you, Detective Vinder."

"Fine. How's the investigation going?"

"Making some progress. You know how it goes. Anyway, do you have a few minutes?"

"Shoot, I've got nothing pressing," Joe said.

"I wanted to revisit our previous conversation. You told me about the Torellos, that gang in Flatbush?"

"Yes, that was their name. That's how I sort of remembered Carlo."

"Yes, well, you thought his name might have been Gino. I just wanted to tell you that you were right. He did go by that name many years ago. Regardless of your little episodes, your memory served you well."

"Oh, I'm not crazy after all," Joe chuckled. "So, he was indeed that character who ran afoul with the mob and us. Was he here as part of a witness protection program?"

"That we do not know, but I believe he just went into hiding about twenty years ago."

"I got it. When you change your name, it's easier to do."

"Right. Until the past two weeks, of course. Carlo's cover was blown, and we're pretty sure it was a hit job."

"Really? That doesn't surprise me, though. The mob never forgets. I remember they were pissed that he worked for himself on their turf."

"But you didn't forget either," Travis said, instantly realizing that it may come over as an insinuation.

"Oh, but that was just pure luck. I mean, the man's face brought that back. Wait, you don't mean..." Joe added hastily.

"No, not at all. I meant to say that your memory of the young Carlo, actually Gino, was correct. Now, who worked his cases? Were you involved?"

"I assume I must have seen him once for some small stuff; when he was pretty young. A Detective O'Grady was more involved when it came to the Torellos and the mob. I'm sure he's retired by now. There were several others, and of course, the guys on the street ran into him all the time."

"He's got quite the record. There's a whole case file on him."

"I'm not surprised. I bet you it became a cold case when Gino disappeared. For all I know, the DA office must have figured he disappeared with the help of the mob."

"No witness protection, then?"

"If he was a cop killer? No way. Hell, no!" Joe said.

"I believe you're right, Joe," Travis said. "But now, we know that his case was closed because he supposedly died on 9/11. I'm getting to take a look at his file tomorrow. Do you recall who in the mob he ran afoul with?"

"That's a tough one. As I said, I didn't handle Gino's case, but I seemed to remember a Gianluca something. Perhaps that was a local boss. I'm sure you will find out tomorrow."

"I hope so. I have one more question for you."

"Shoot."

'If the mob were to send a hitman after him, they must have known that he was moving here. The reason I'm saying that is because our murder suspect moved here two months earlier, setting up shop under a fake name. Any experience in this?"

Joe thought for a while, and all Travis heard for a time was a humming sound. Then Joe spoke up: "Maybe Carlo wasn't his target initially. Carlo just walked into it. Have you thought of that?"

It was now Travis' turn to be quiet. Indeed, he hadn't considered it at all. Another target in this neighborhood seemed most unlikely, he figured. "No, I haven't," he answered. "That would be too much of a coincidence. It also begs the question of why our suspect didn't kill this initial target as well."

"Hey, detective," Joe laughed at the other end. "You're the detective now; I'm retired."

"Right you are," Travis said. "Thanks, I'll let you know something when I figure all this out."

Travis walked back into his living room, where Maureen was reading. "I need to check with Ramón quickly, and then I'll be back," he said. "I'd like to turn in early tonight because I have to leave around five."

Maureen looked up and smiled. "Yes, dear. I'm looking forward to some extra rest time."

Chapter 28

New York City

Travis checked his notes on the flight to Newark. Ramón and the officers had found the motel that Jerry stayed in for about two months. The dates corresponded with those of the car rental, and Travis wasn't surprised. He paid with the same credit card, and a check with Citi Card had confirmed the validity of the card and the fact that it was issued about three months ago. Ramón had inquired about the address associated with the Visa card, and it matched the one on the driver's license. Again, all seemed above board and correct. However, the street address didn't belong to a person named Jerry Darcay; instead, it belonged to a Roger Bonelli. That was the kind of information that made Travis love his job. It was a valuable piece of a puzzle, and it needed inspection later today.

Patrick had arranged Travis' contact in the City. More specifically, he would drive directly to retired detective O'Grady's home and learn more about Gino Barese. In the afternoon, he would be visiting the precinct and spend time looking through the paperwork.

The drive into the city took him longer than expected, especially when he had a late start because of some confusion at the car rental place. He pulled into the Prospect Heights neighborhood off Flatbush Avenue and was pleasantly surprised to see the tree-lined streets. He stopped in front of the house number Patrick had given him.

Paddy O'Grady was a tall septuagenarian with almost perfect white hair and matching mustache. With a firm handshake, he welcomed Travis into his flat. "Come in, detective. How's my old buddy Joe doing in North Carolina?" he laughed.

"Joe's fine, enjoying retirement and our warmer weather," Travis replied as they walked into a big living room where one entire wall had become a bookcase. "Thanks for taking the time, by the way."

"Oh, no problem. Your weather's just too humid and hot for me, and I can't subject my Irish blood to that."

"I gotcha," Travis said and sat down on the couch that Paddy motioned him to.

"So, I hear that Gino Barese died, again," Paddy said. "Patrick told me all about it. How can I help you?"

"I'm going through his case file later today, but I want to learn as much as possible about Gino. I believe that his story may contain a clue as to why someone sent a hitman."

"I'm not that familiar with his early years, although over time we interviewed a lot of relatives who can give you a better insight. I remember that he was already in trouble at a very young age. Not just the small, petty things kids do, but more serious things that would raise red flags. Of course, I didn't get involved until he became a gang member and later worked for the mob. It wasn't until the turn of the century that he messed up by getting in trouble with the Fortimare family. You probably already know that he ran afoul with one of the bosses, right?

"Yes, I was told. Can you tell me exactly how he pissed off the mob?"

"Simple. He killed someone in the family. He got away with it but only because he would be a valuable source for us in the family. "

"Did you work that case with Joe?"

"Not really. We talked about it, I believe. I'm sure his recollection's as good as mine. Anyway, at one point, Gino became an informant. We thought we had the perfect in, but Gino had other motives. When the undercover cop in charge was on to him, he either killed him or had him killed. When that happened, we were all over this criminal. He had nowhere to turn. The mob and the DA both wanted to get this guy off the street. The mafia had a straightforward plan; we had a different process in mind. If you're looking for a motive, there's only one. The goons couldn't find him then, but they didn't forget. When word on the street was that Gino died in the Towers, we closed our case. Somehow someone in the family got wind of the same thing you uncovered. Gino was alive and well, and then he gave up his safe haven and moved to your state. They located him and took care of him. If you're looking for a motive, there's no other."

"I'd figured that by now. Has anyone worked on the case since 9/11?"

"I doubt it. As I said, the case was closed within a year. When you get to see the documents, take a look to see if someone has checked the file since then."

"That's a grand idea. One never knows," Travis nodded. "Now, I was interested in learning more about Gino."

"Why is that necessary? Once you read his file, you will find out all you need to know."

"It's the nuances I'm looking to find out. Gino's younger years will not reveal much, maybe, but I'm still intrigued by the character who became a criminal and then walked away from it for about two decades. I also owe some explanation to a family in Scranton."

"I get it. I think I can help you with Gino, the kid. I believe one of his aunts still lives here in the neighborhood. We interviewed her a very long time ago, and I recognized her when I went to a farmer's market a few months ago."

"Great. Perhaps I can do that before I go to the precinct."

"Sure, I'll get her information," Paddy said as he walked to the kitchen area.

Travis checked his phone. It was after ten, and still, there was no message from Ramón. The search for Jerry and Roger had not turned up anything.

Paddy returned with a handwritten note. Travis was surprised to see a telephone number. "Now, that's handy. Do you mind if I give her a call?"

"No, go right ahead," Paddy said.

Travis stood up and walked toward a window overlooking the street. The phone rang for a while, and a woman answered. "Hello?"

"Hello, yes, is this Lucille Conti?" Travis asked.

"Yes, who's this? I don't buy over the phone."

"No worry. I'm with the police in North Carolina and visiting with a detective O'Grady here."

"Oh, I know the fellah," she said. "Saw him not too long ago. Is this about my nephew again?"

"I'm afraid so," Travis sighed. "Too much to go over on the phone, I'm afraid. I'm particularly interested in his younger years, and Paddy O'Grady told me you could probably share some memories about Gino's years as a kid."

"Are you writing a book or something?" Lucille asked.

"Oh no," Travis chuckled. "I'm just doing some background checking for a case I'm working on."

"Oh, I see. When do you want to talk to me?"

"Maybe in a half hour or so. It won't last very long," Travis assured her.

"Do you have my address?"

"I do. See you in a short while then?"

"Okay. What's your name again?"

"Sorry, forgot that one. My name is Travis Vinder."

When he returned to the couch, Paddy looked quizzically. "You're not going to tell her about the identity switch, are you?"

"Not planning on it," Travis confirmed. "No point in that. I doubt the murder in North Carolina will make the papers here."

"I agree," Paddy said. "So, what else would you like to know?"

"Everything you remember about your contacts with Gino, his arrests, and especially all you know about the gang he belonged to and his connections with the mob here."

"All that in a half-hour?"

"We can do it, Paddy," Travis said. "I'll ask a set of questions, and we'll be done in no time."

Paddy got comfortable, and Travis got out his notebook after turning his phone to silent mode.

Chapter 29

Young Gino

Travis found the apartment quickly using the GPS on his phone. He rang once, and the door opened immediately. Lucille wore a summer dress with a dense floral pattern. Perhaps she'd applied too much makeup, but generally, she looked great for someone in her eighties.

"Come in, detective," she said.

Travis stepped inside and waited for Lucille to close the door. "Thanks for seeing me at such short notice," he said and let her go ahead in the small hallway. The living room was tiny and overstuffed with couches, chairs, and two tables. No doubt, family heirlooms that she'd never dared to sell or give away.

"So, young man," Lucille said while opening a window to a back alley. "Please sit down. Can I get you a cup of coffee? I just made a fresh pot."

"Sure," Travis said and picked a single upholstered chair. "I'll take it black, thank you."

A few moments later, Lucille returned with a small tray, shaking the cup slightly as she put it down on a small side table. "What's the case you're working on?"

Travis realized that the older woman wasn't just going to give up her information freely. She was genuinely interested. He decided to walk a fine line. "Your nephew's case came to my attention when we were investigating a criminal investigation regarding a man named Carlo Messina."

"Never heard of him, I'm sorry," Lucille said, sipping water from a glass.

"That's no problem," Travis smiled. "It's just that he's connected with Gino in the past. So, can you tell me a bit about Gino and how he grew up?"

"Sure. I still have a sharp mind. I can start when little Gino was about five or so, is that okay?"

Travis nodded and opened his notebook, while Lucille adjusted her dress, making sure her knees were adequately covered.

"My sister Angie, Gino's mother, didn't have an easy time with her children. For that matter, I didn't either, but we had different outcomes, I guess. She was taking care of their youngest, Annamarie, while Gino was at school. Just before the school bus came back with the kids, Angie would start her routine. She'd put on a fresh layer of Revlon Cherries in the Snow lipstick. Then Angie would scoop up Annamarie from her playpen and run across the street just in time for the school bus. She never had time to chat with the other moms. Gino usually bounced down the steps resembling A.A. Milne's Tigger more than a five-year-old. Of course, Angie thought her son was so adorable, brown curly hair, huge brown eyes framed by the longest eyelashes, he looked cherubic. His behavior wasn't so angelic."

"Angelic, you said?" Travis couldn't resist.

"Yes. I once visited, and all little Gino said when entering the house was "Spaghetti and meatballs!" The house smelled super yummy, and it was Gino's favorite for dinner. I couldn't believe she gave him three Mallomars and a glass of milk. At least Annamarie got a regular bottle of milk. I guess he always changed his clothes to go outside and claimed he was going to ride his bike. Gino usually had other ideas. One day I saw him go out, but he walked across the hood, roof, and trunk of an old Chevy parked in front of the house next door. Gino tried a few jumps, the Chevy bounced, the neighbor came barreling off the porch, screaming curses as Gino ran into his backyard, slamming the gate. I'm sure this wasn't the first unpleasant interaction with adults. The kid hated animals, cats, and dogs in particular. He always called them stupid and threw rocks at them. Then again, he thought that most people were stupid too."

"I guess his mother didn't keep a close eye on him. How about his father?"

Gino's dad, Nicky, traveled the Long Island Railroad between Manhattan and the Massapequa train station. Many people did that in those days, so they only needed one car, living so close to the station. Nicky had served on the aircraft carrier, the USS Shangri-La, as an airplane mechanic, hoping to land a TWA or PanAm job after the war. It wasn't to be, and Nicky worked in the zoning department for the City of New York. Massapequa was a post-World War II community populated by former GIs and their young families. Gino grew up in this world. New schools were popping up all over the town. Despite these efforts, all the schools were bursting at the seams. Gino's grandparents lived in Brooklyn and had no intention of relocating to Massapequa, or elsewhere on Long Island.

The Bareses lived in a neat cape cod with three bedrooms, one bathroom, a living room, a dining room, and an eat-in kitchen. Angie longed to live in one of the waterfront houses, maybe on a canal. She only said that because my husband and I, together with our two sons, lived on the waterfront."

"So, you could afford that at the time?" Travis asked. "What kind of work did your husband do?"

Lucille fidgeted a bit but answered firmly. "My husband was *connected* as we called it then, but Nicky would have no part of mob life. He was happy with his GI house, his pretty wife, his two healthy kids, and not being in the Navy anymore. He was less happy with his job and that daily trek into the city, I tell you that!" Lucille said and took another sip.

"How did Angie fare with Gino?" Travis asked.

"As I said, Gino wasn't what you would call *an easy* child. Angie called him her wild child. He wasn't a great student despite Angie's best efforts to get him to do his homework, practice his spelling, and read a book now and then. When Annamarie started school, things were different. She did her homework, studied her spelling, read countless books. As she got older, she read every Nancy Drew she could get her hands on. Gino hated school, struggled with reading; the letters in his primer were a jumbled mess and made no sense. Gino's handwriting was even worse, and even he couldn't decipher what he wrote. Although Gino pretended not to care, he told Angie that school was stupid. I figured that Gino pretty much decided to give up trying."

"How did your family get along with your sister's family?"

"Generally great. I had two boys, Joey and Vinnie. They were a bit older and quite wild too. Most Sundays, our two families gathered at our house after church service for a fabulous Italian feast. Lasagna, chicken parmesan, chicken piccata, braciola, sausage and peppers, chicken cacciatore, the list goes on and on. Sometimes Angie's and my parents joined us, bringing cannolis and sfogliatelle cookies from Brooklyn, or homemade struffoli. Gino and his cousins always had a grand old time, running amuck in the fancy neighborhood. Annamarie stuck to safety near us, the adults."

"How did your sons get along with Gino?"

"It all looked normal. Many years later, we discovered that the three had formed a club or *gang,* as they called it. They used red permanent markers to draw "tattoos" with devil horns on their upper arms. I also found out that, when they were about eight or nine years old, they rode their bikes to the deli. Gino apparently sat on the back of Vinnie's bike. When they came out with their baseball cards, there was a new, black, three-speed Schwinn just lying on the sidewalk. Joey and Vinnie encouraged Gino to hop on and go, and he did." It seemed Joey cooed to Gino that he was a loyal gang member. The boys rode back to the house at top speed, and they stowed Gino's new bike in the garage with the others. I'm sure Gino thought he'd gotten away with the theft. As parents, we never asked too many questions, not with the line of work Joe Sr. was doing."

"Do you believe that is how he started on a criminal path?"

"I guess so. My husband, who was known in the business as Rocky, started by stealing and collecting dues from small shopkeepers. For protection, they called it. Everyone has a beginning somewhere."

"How about you and Angie's parents?"

"Angie was the one that complained to our mother about her frustrations with Gino. All she got as an answer was that she should send the children to Catholic school, the nuns would keep him in line. Angie told me that it was a nonstarter. She said no Catholic school for her kids, no rulers on the knuckles. Somehow Angie did know her son would get into trouble sooner or later," Lucille said. She got up and checked Travis' cup.

"A refill?"

"Sure," Travis said.

Lucille took the tray and returned with a fresh cup of coffee and a refilled glass of water.

"So, that bike thing happened when he was about eight or so. What kind of trouble did he get into later?"

"By the time Gino was in fourth grade, he'd become a big bully in school. He didn't get into too many fights; the other boys were already too afraid to engage. He didn't get invited to many birthday parties or sleepovers at his classmate's homes. His peers shied away from him more and more, and he became angrier. Gino continued to do poorly in school, and he didn't get promoted to sixth grade. It took a while before Angie told me all that. Naturally, he was the tallest in his class for fifth and sixth grades. He acted like a thug as he strutted around. Gino attracted a lot of attention from the girls in his class, but the boys were mostly afraid of him. I think Gino felt embarrassed having to repeat a year in school. Angie said he felt stupid. As you can imagine, Gino never shared these feelings of inadequacy with anyone; he might not be smart, but he was still very, very cool. Joey and Vinnie said that Gino believed he owned the school. The three always hung out together every Sunday, and Gino rode 'his' black Schwinn through the ritzy neighborhood. No one ever asked about the bike. One day, the cousins rode up to a large house right on the Great South Bay. Joey boasted that the mafia kingpin lived there. Joey was proud to share that my husband worked for the big boss. If it scared Gino, I don't know, but he quickly learned that cops weren't looking for stolen bikes.

All the boys grew into handsome young men, but of the three, Gino was by far the best looking. Vinnie told me that in Junior High, some of the hoodie girls were calling him the Italian stallion, but not to his face. I heard him talking one night to Joey, and he said that Gino occasionally stole a kiss on the playground. Angie confessed that Gino never asked for money because his shoplifting skills were quite sophisticated. He loved the movie West Side Story and fancied himself a gang member, much like the Jets. It was like 'When you're a Jet, you're a Jet all the way, from your first cigarette to your last dying day.' I'm sure he smoked all through Junior High."

Travis had remained quiet until he figured Lucille would have to come up for air soon. He was surprised she knew so much about Gino. She and her sister most likely talked about their sons often, knowing that all three were a handful. She took a sip of water. "So, if he didn't have money, where did he get his cigarettes?" Travis asked.

"Cigarettes were a bit hard to steal since they were usually behind the counter. As far as I remember, Gino did manage to steal them because he always had a pack in his sleeve. He may have been *cool* as they called it, but being just cool in school didn't mean he was a good student."

"Did he go on to High School?"

"Interesting that you should ask. You see, Nicky wasn't pleased with his son's grades, his cocky attitude, and the fact that he often reeked of cigarette smoke. The calls from the principal were disturbing. Gino shook down kids for money, started fights when someone didn't fall into step. Gino was often grounded. Angie and Nicky had constant arguments about their oldest child. They loved their children, and neither knew how to rein Gino in. So far, Gino had not gotten into any real trouble involving the police. Little did the Bareses know that was because he was a very cunning little crook. He simply hadn't been caught yet. Unfortunately, my sons only encouraged him to follow their lead. They were no angels and destined to follow in their father's footsteps. They were lousy role models for Gino," Lucille said. She took a big gulp of water and continued.

"Gino's last year in Junior High was a good one for him. Being a year older than most kids added to the swagger, bravado, cursing, and overconfidence. 'Pride cometh before the fall,' I say. So, Whelan's Drugs had an impressive display of cigarettes behind the counter, but not too far behind the counter. The temptation was too much to resist, with Joey and Vinnie egging Gino to "do it," but his luck ran out. Being chauffeured home in the back of a Nassau County police car wasn't his finest moment. Needless to say, his parents were displeased. No charges were filed at that time, just a warning that it wouldn't go so well with the law the next time. Not only was Gino grounded, but his dad also took away his record player, records, radio, television, and telephone access for a month.

The event proved to be the final straw. Nicky Barese had decided that the family would be moving out of harm's way, away from the delinquent cousins and hoodlum posse of Massapequa, out of New York and into the Garden State. Nicky had been jumping through hoops to become an air traffic controller at Newark Airport. Even Angie didn't know about his plans until he had the job. As the school year was ending, my sister was heartbroken by the news. Angie was sad, but Nicky insisted. If Gino went to Massapequa High School, he wouldn't be around his cousins every day. I knew that Nicky thought I had a bad influence on Angie. Nothing was further from the truth," Lucille said, shaking her head. She took a deep breath and continued.

"Yes, I always strutted around in outrageous outfits, flashing ostentatious makeup and jewelry. I think Nicky was fearful and didn't want Angie to end up like me. Anyway, their cute little cape cod sold in a flash, and when school ended, they moved to New Jersey. Only Nicky was happy, Angie and Annamarie sulked and cried. Gino stomped, slammed doors, and looked sullen and mean, snapping and cursing. Gino threatened to run away, but on moving day, he climbed into the back seat of the family station wagon under his father's piercing stare. Angie later told me that the drive to New Jersey was silent except for Nicky's humming a few times. I didn't see them again for about ten years when we all showed up for a wedding. By then, we'd grown apart, and only Angie and I talked. My husband wouldn't let me get close to the family anymore. Mob rules, he called it."

"Wow," Travis said. "Quite a story of young Gino. I believe it sets the stage to understand what happened in the following years."

"Yeah, well, like my sons, good for nothing. All three joined my husband working for the Fortimare family."

"What are your husband and sons doing now, Mrs. Conti?'

'Joe Sr. died of cancer in ninety-five, and Junior has been in jail since 1998. Vinnie went to college and became an accountant. He went to work for an insurance company that was a front for la Familia. Of course, you know about Gino."

"I'm so sorry it turned out like that."

"Nah, don't you worry. I'm happy where I am, and I can easily live off my income."

Travis got up. "Well, Lucille, thanks for sharing your stories. I'm just curious, but do you happen to know the name of the insurance company Vinnie works for?"

"Oh, that. I believe it's called Bonelli and Partners. They had an office in one of the twin towers in the City, you know. Nowadays, they have a nice spread on Flatbush. Vinnie is a VP now. Don't see him much, though."

"Good to know. Thanks for the info. Have a great day and don't worry, I'll let myself out."

Chapter 30

Bonelli & Partners

A quick check for directions on his phone led Travis directly to the office building that housed Bonelli & Partners. He was quite aware that he had no jurisdiction, but perhaps a revised accounting of the death of Gino Barese might get him to see his cousin. The parking lot next to the building made it easy to park off the busy avenue.

The three-story building stood out from other buildings nearby because of its expensive marble looking exterior. It seemed to belong in a more upscale business park. Marble-looking statues, some headless, lined the long and wide lobby area. They were undoubtedly facsimiles of their ancient Roman counterparts. Travis mused that it appeared fitting for la Familia to honor their ancestral roots. An expansive wooden table served as the reception desk. A uniformed guard looked up from a screen as Travis lightly coughed to attract his attention. He saw a multitude of screens behind the man, showing what cameras at various locations in the building recorded.

"Can I help you?" the man asked.

"Sure. I'm here to see Mr. Conti."

"Do you have an appointment?"

"I'm afraid I don't. I just visited with his mother around the corner, and she suggested I stop by to share some family news with him.

The man looked puzzled. "Mr. Vinnie has family nearby? News to me. Anyway, let me look at his appointments today. What's your name again?"

Travis decided against using his badge to speed up the process and not scare off the man. "Travis Vinder."

"Does he know you?"

"I'm afraid not. You tell Mr. Conti I'm here regarding Gino Barese. I'm sure he'll see me."

The man slightly shrugged his shoulders and pushed a few buttons on his keyboard. Travis took the time to look at some of the screens. One showed him standing at the table while others displayed empty hallways. He heard the man talk to someone. "Ok, I'll send him up."

Travis nodded. "Okay, thanks."

"Take the elevator to the third floor. Mr. Conti's assistant will see you there."

Once in the elevator, Travis noticed the date of installation: November 22, 2002. The door opened, and a young woman in a black mini dress welcomed him. "Mr. Vinnie will see you in a minute." She took him to a small conference room and left. The sparsely decorated room seemed sterile and unwelcoming. Travis imagined that perhaps more affluent clients got to meet in a different place. He decided to stand by the window through which he had a perfect view of the parking lot.

Vinnie Conti walked in seconds later. He was a large man of medium height, nearly bald. Over his starched white shirt, he wore black suspenders holding up black slacks. He held a pair of glasses in his right hand. Travis took that to be a sign that the man wasn't about to shake hands, indicating he had little time for this interruption. "Your name is Vinder? Have we met?"

"Travis Vinder. No, we haven't," Travis answered.

"What business did you have with my mother?"

"Oh, I was doing some background checking on Gino Barese, you know, your cousin."

"I'm sure she had nothing to tell you about him. Anyway, he's dead. I'm not sure why you're here."

"Actually, I'm a detective with the Durham Police Department in North Carolina, and I'm investigating the murder of Gino Barese."

Vinnie laughed out loud. "That's a good one. He's been dead for almost twenty years, and you're investigating that now? Do you guys have too much time that you can waste it on something like that?"

"We investigate all murders, and this one happened this week," Travis said. He was a bit surprised the man didn't react to the word 'murder.'

"Now, that's a joke, right? Gino died in the Towers. You're wasting your time."

"We have proof that he didn't and took a different name. He went underground and appeared in North Carolina a few weeks ago."

"Interesting story, Mr. Vinder, but it has nothing to do with me."

"I didn't imply it did. I just wanted you to know what happened. Although you and your family believe that Gino died a long time ago, you have the right to know what really happened to him."

"Yeah, well, in the end, it doesn't change anything, does it?" Vinnie said. "Thanks for stopping by. Good luck with your investigation, detective," Vinnie said and grabbed the door handle.

"Oh, rest assured, we'll find out who murdered your cousin and why, but I agree we need some good luck. You see, I believe that Gino Barese's earlier life holds clues to his murder."

"Good for you."

"I do have another question for you if I may?" Travis asked.

"I can't possibly help you," Vinnie said, opening the door wider.

"Did Bonelli & Partners have offices at the World Trade Center in September of 2001?"

Travis noticed a slight loosening of the man's grip on the door handle. The hesitation in answering was more apparent. "Why would this matter?" Vinnie stumbled.

"Isn't it true that Gino was meeting with you or someone in your company on that September 11th? At least it seems from your appointment ledger that he had a meeting at your office that day."

The door closed.

"Why would that matter?"

"Were you in the building that day?"

"No, I wasn't. Lucky, I guess. Listen, Mr. Vinder, I don't think I can help you here. But hey, thanks for the updated news on my cousin. I trust my mother wasn't too upset hearing that?"

"Oh, I never told her. You know, I didn't want to bring all that sorry business about the attack on the World Trade Center and the death of her nephew up again."

"I see," Vinnie said, suddenly in deep thought. He reached for the door handle. "Well, maybe that was smart of you. Thanks."

Travis had just one more question, which was prompted by Vinnie's not being at his office in the South Tower that fateful day. "Did anyone from your office escape from the building that day?"

"Yeah, everyone did. They were very smart to leave right away."

"I see, and that's when you guys moved in here?"

"The building was going to be a bank, but we were able to buy it, and we moved in a year later."

"Well, that turned out to be good then," Travis smiled. "It's a nice place, by the way."

"Thanks. Well, have a good trip back to North Carolina. Durham, right?"

Travis noticed the forced casual tone. It was as if Vinnie wanted to stress that he wasn't familiar with the place. Travis had a feeling the opposite was true. "One more question, and I swear, I'm out of your hair."

Vinnie guided Travis out of the room. In the hallway, in front of the elevator, he turned to Vinnie. "Did Gino work for your company, or was he working for himself?"

"Gino never worked for anyone, detective. Gino was his own boss if you must know. He may have been a wise guy at times, but he was smart."

"That's what I figured," Travis agreed. "Oh, I almost forgot to ask. Does a Roger Bonelli work here?"

Vinnie pressed the button, and without looking up, he said: "Our old boss. He's long retired. Why do you ask?"

"Oh, it's just that a fellow I talked to in Durham called him here a few weeks ago."

"Impossible, he left over four years ago."

"So, if someone called for Roger, who would have taken the call?"

"The receptionist, for sure," Vinnie said as he held the elevator door open.

"I see," Travis said as he stepped in. "Well, thanks for your time."

Travis was convinced that the insurance company was somehow involved in the 'why' and 'who' in the case. Mr. Whitman had a connection with an old boss, Jerry's address was listed here, and Gino was linked through his cousin. Not only that, but Vinnie had also given him a big clue when he said that the employees got out of the building. Others at the firm must have seen Gino get out as well that day and perhaps seen him head for Mike's cab. Maybe they walked out as a group. It was clear that even in all the confusion of rushing down the stairs and out into the street, at least one employee knew that Gino wasn't one of the victims that day. Undoubtedly, Vinnie must have been told about it, and he and his bosses had to know that Gino had escaped from both the tragedy and a previous life. Both had been necessary for Gino to stay alive.

Chapter 31

Gino's Career

Travis drove into Manhattan, cursing the traffic like a regular. His conversation with Vinnie had been enlightening. It bothered him that Vinnie Conti hadn't reacted to the news about Gino's murder the way he would have expected. If Vinnie had been convinced that Gino died on 9/11, he would've protested the fact that Gino was killed in Durham. Travis didn't buy the feigned unfamiliarity with Durham. It was most likely that Vinnie knew that Gino had moved to Carolina Arbors. In any case, he'd rattled the cage, and soon he'd have to involve the local colleagues.

The downtown office was chaotic. Fortunately, the file on Gino Barese was ready in a small office, and Travis had full access. He sat down and turned over the faded yellow cover of the extra thick folder. Someone had typed up a summary of the case file on Mr. Barese. It appeared the author had pulled his information from the documents underneath that constituted the pile of papers.   Perhaps this was the last act of the case before it was closed. Travis started to read.

Gino Barese became a troublesome teenager and was arrested several times for stealing. Nothing severe or enough to warrant a Juve conviction. Right out of High School, he enjoyed the benefits of working for his uncle Rocky. Whenever interrogated for something, Gino never used the word uncle. It was apparent that he had moved on from petty theft to more serious crimes under the guidance of la Familia. He got more and more responsibility and was getting better at not endangering his minor position. During a talk with him in the late seventies, it was noted that he was anxious to live the good life. His uncle must have paid him well, but it wasn't enough for him to afford a nice place yet, and he seemed to strive for a comfortable social life. He was into women.

Travis had the impression that so far, Gino's career, if you can call it that, was pretty much an extension of the life his aunt Lucille had revealed. As he continued reading, there was a knock on the door. A skinny looking grey-haired man sporting a three-day beard reached his hand toward Travis. "Sergeant Byrne. You are Travis, I assume?"

Travis nodded and shook hands. "Travis Vinder, yes, Sergeant."

"Call me John," the man said.

"Thanks for getting the file ready for me," Travis said.

"No problem. I've known Patrick for years, and that's the least I can do. You see, I never got anything to stick on this Barese character. We sort of had a dual relationship, you see."

"How's that?"

"Well, on the one hand, he was a suspect in many cases, but with the help of mob lawyers, got off, and on the other hand, he was a snitch that I used to catch bigger fish."

"I get that, but I was just reading here that..."

"I know what's in the file. I wrote that summary," John said. "I can save you the time reading through the thirty pages and give you sort of a synopsis. If you need to look at a specific incident later, we can always do that."

"Sounds like a plan," Travis said and pushed the file aside, making room for his notebook. "So, tell me about the young Gino, he was a womanizer I gathered."

John grabbed a chair and sat down. "Oh, yes. You can say that again. He was seen with several women but didn't appear to get serious with any of them. Dating and casual sex were probably more what he wanted at that point in his life. He exhibited the common fear of all young mobsters that he would have to explain what he did for a living if he got too involved. Officers had heard on the street that he told girls that he was in finance. That wasn't a total lie, but he declined to elaborate where his money originated. During several raids on nightclubs, he was seen with women, spending a lot of money."

"I see," Travis said. "So what prompted him to go from stealing a bike and other things to more serious offenses?"

"Basically, women. The first time Gino Barese made a big mistake was when he tried to impress a new girl he wanted to snag. He started bragging about how he had friends in powerful places. In this area, that usually meant only one thing, the Mob. Someone overheard him talking about it in one of the local bars, and it got back to his boss. We heard about Gino being summoned to Rocky's office. He must have been concerned but probably didn't know about the purpose of the meeting. We found out that when Rocky came into the room, he was boiling mad. "How could you be so stupid?" Rocky screamed. "You don't go around bragging about working for me."

Gino tried to explain, to no avail. Rocky told him that he never wanted this to happen again, and if it did, there would be dire consequences. The business needed people who knew how to keep secrets, including the fact that they worked for the family. Impressing a woman was no excuse for such behavior. He told Gino that if all he wanted was a beautiful woman for sex, he had plenty of them working for him. He suggested that his nephew should refrain from picking up women in bars for the foreseeable future."

"I bet Gino didn't care much for that suggestion?"

"Oh, you are right. He complained about being mistreated. He'd been working for Rocky for almost four years, and in all that time, he'd never done anything to make the boss question his loyalty. One stupid comment shouldn't have resulted in such a reaction. When I heard this from one of our undercover agents, I figured the young man would heed Rocky's warning. Not so: Gino was no longer as happy to be in his employ as before. We discussed at the time how that could turn into an advantage for us."

"So, what happened next?" Travis wondered.

"We knew that Gino was in the business of extracting so-called dues from local shops. There were many confrontations, but over the years, this protection was sold as insurance. The mob family that his uncle worked for used an insurance company as a front. So, in effect, Gino was an insurance salesman. The difference with regular insurance companies was that the mob's insurance plan never paid anything out. So, over the years, Gino kept his nose clean, ensuring that everything was okay with his uncle and that the dues kept coming. We figured he was still harboring resentment, but it wasn't yet time to do something about it. We had to wait for Gino to make the first move. However, that didn't happen, because, at some point, he must have hatched a plan in which he would keep his job, but would also make some additional money on the side. I guess he was still anxious to improve his lifestyle. To make his plan work, he needed to collect money from businesses that weren't insured yet. He couldn't afford to siphon money away from existing customers because Rocky kept tight books."

"That side business surely got him in trouble with Rocky."

"Not right away. You see, there were many businesses where Gino didn't collect any payments, and he wondered why they didn't have to pay. He looked into why a few were allowed to escape the paid protection insurance. Gino chose some of the smaller ones and began by asking simple questions about them when he met with other collectors. He found out that some of the shops were owned by people who had connections to someone that was a part of the organization. That freed them from payments. Also, some had ties to people in the law enforcement community, and it wasn't worth the risk to pressure them into payment. Rocky had several local cops on his payroll, but not enough to ensure his complete safety if he chose to intimidate the wrong people."

"So, he started to shake them down anyway?"

"Gino decided that a great way to get extra money would be to contact some of the businesses that were not paying protection insurance. Acting as if he was representing the family, he got them to start paying for protection. He kept a separate ledger for these companies and, of course, kept the money for himself. He did his homework, though, and made sure there were no conflicts. We are confident that this drove his extra activities more to the outskirts of town, where many businesses suited him perfectly."

"And how did that work out?"

"As far as we learned, the following year, Gino spent a lot of his free time frequenting some of the businesses that he thought might be easy and profitable targets. He kept a low profile as he didn't want to run into any problems when he confronted the owners about protection. When Gino decided the time was right, he approached the owner of a diner. He was surprised when the owner told him that he was expecting this eventually and would not give him any problems as long as the payments were reasonable. The owner told us that he let Gino know that he'd already been contacted by someone at the time he purchased the diner. He was forced to buy all his supplies from the "right" companies. Nevertheless, the owner agreed to a certain amount, and Gino must have been pleased."

"So, he felt cocky and tried some other businesses?"

"You guessed that right. That same day he went to a pet store, but the owner wasn't on the premises. He ran into the same problem at a Laundromat. However, I believe that the events at the Chinese restaurant made him rethink his plan. I'm convinced that he wasn't sure how well that would go as most people there didn't speak much English. Gino gave it a try. He asked to see the owner, who did speak some English. He started to explain why he was there, and the man went ballistic. He started screaming at him in Chinese, and two men from the back came out, and he was physically thrown out of the restaurant."

"And did he rethink his plan?"

"He must have convinced himself to persist. I'm sure he'd made them realize he was working for the mob, but if a few more folded, his confidence would grow. He probably wondered how, in the past, Rocky managed to get so many of the businesses to pay protection. Maybe he sent a couple of his big goons out to intimidate them. Now, as you know, Gino wasn't a terrifying-looking person and didn't inspire fear in anyone, and that would need to change. He figured that carrying a gun would help. He ended up talking to Rocky about getting one. He told one of our detectives that he sold Rocky on the idea because some areas where he collected were getting a bit sketchy. He must have told his uncle that he didn't want to lose any collections by getting robbed," John paused.

'I see where this is heading," Travis said. "I assume he did get a gun and used it?"

John nodded. He seemed lost in thoughts for a minute as if recounting all that they had learned. "I gather Rocky wasn't surprised by Gino's request to carry a gun, but Gino had to be trained in not only how to use it, but how to care for it. Rocky, a careful crook, would get Gino a non-traceable gun. We assumed he got the weapon shortly afterward because we have records of him using it at a Newark firing range. Gino never owned or fired a gun before that."

"Did someone teach him how to use it?" Travis asked.

"Yes, a fellow named Carlos gave him all the instruction he needed: how to load the gun, shoot it, and clean it. From then on, he went to the range weekly. I'm sure he was comfortable with it after a while."

"And probably more than what he needed on his job."

"We think so. From interrogating Carlos a year later, we knew that Gino was aware of the laws for carrying a gun in Brooklyn and New Jersey. It was required to have a concealed carry permit. Carlos told Gino that he should keep it in the glove compartment or trunk of his car for now and advised him not to get a permit. Doing so would risk a background check, and if the authorities discovered that he worked for Rocky, there could be problems. We know that Gino wasn't worried about getting a concealed carry permit. He bought a shoulder holster so he could carry the weapon under his jacket. This way, if someone gave him a hard time, he could just ease back his jacket so the gun became visible. With that scenario in place, Gino must have figured that the gun gave him more of a tough guy status. He thought he could approach some new businesses and casually flash the weapon to see if he could get more protection money. He knew it was risky, but he wanted to make some big money for himself."

"So, this was an essential change in addressing those new customers."

"It sure was. Caldwell had some definite possibilities among the nearby towns in Jersey, so he started frequenting a couple of them to get a feel for the places. He decided that a small mom and pop restaurant was a great place to start. Gino approached the man that he thought was the owner. He explained who he was and how the payments would work. He was surprised at how easy it was, and they settled on terms. Maybe this new territory was the answer to his greed. Next, he approached a bar and tavern in the same neighborhood. Gino had no way of knowing that this was going to be one of the biggest mistakes of his life."

"Did all this happen before he became an informer for you guys?"

"Yes. Gino hadn't been scared enough yet to run away from the mob and into our arms. Now, about that bar, Marty's Pub. It was owned by one of Rocky's cousins. The owner didn't react at all when Gino explained to him why he was there. He told him he was the manager and would have to talk to the owner and get back to him. Gino tried to act tough and threatened trouble if the manager didn't cooperate. He said he would get back to him by the next day. Gino left feeling confident and decided to treat himself to a nice dinner with one of the girls he knew. You can already guess what happened. During dinner, he was summoned to Rocky's office the second time. He had no idea what his uncle had in store for him. When he arrived, Gino was met by one of Rocky's lieutenants, Mikey Freese, and was taken to a room in the building's basement. He waited for over a half an hour, and when Rocky walked in, he must have known by the look on his uncle's face that he was in trouble. We don't know how the conversation went, but I guess Rocky asked him how business was going. It was a form of laying the groundwork, knowing how Rocky operated. At one point, Gino must have denied pressing any other companies for payment, not knowing that Rocky already knew. Gino didn't realize that there was another collector for Rocky operating in Caldwell. We know that Gino was stubborn and most likely didn't come clean. I'm sure that Marty's Pub came up, and that's when Gino realized he was in a bad spot. Pleading for mercy wasn't going to soften Rocky. Family or not, Gino's time had come."

"We know that Rocky didn't kill him, so what happened?"

"The usual stuff. Take Gino out in the rear seat of a car, making him sweat bullets as he figured he would be shot. Gino still had his gun. I can't believe that his uncle's goons hadn't checked him for a weapon. They probably thought he was no threat to them. The story goes that once they were out of town, heading toward the Meadowlands, Gino pulled out his gun. He shot Tony, the guy next to him, in the chest and then put the weapon to the back of Mikey's head. Gino told Mikey to pull the car over and get out. He then climbed into the front seat and took off. Minutes later, police officers spotted Mikey walking on the shoulder of the freeway. Mikey's story about a man he gave a ride to and who pulled a gun on him was a bit shady. They found an unregistered weapon on him and handcuffed him.

Once they put him in the back of the patrol car, Mikey revealed that he shot out his car's rear window as it was taking off. The officers followed the freeway and caught up with Gino, who thought he'd gotten away. It didn't take long to put two and two together, and Gino couldn't explain the dying man in the back seat. He decided his only way out was to tell what happened. Gino told the officers that he worked for Rocky. He'd gotten in trouble with Rocky, and two of his enforcers took him out to kill him. He had a gun on him and used it to get away, and claimed the shooting was in self-defense."

"So, now he's in trouble with the law and with Rocky. How did he ever get out of that? When did that happen?"

"I think it was in '95. Anyway, Gino and Mikey were brought in and questioned. Tony died in the hospital."

"So, Gino killed a mafia lieutenant and violated their turf. Good reasons to kill him. Perhaps, still a basis for murder after twenty years."

"That would be a motive, but after all these years?"

"The mob never forgives or forgets; you know that," Travis said.

"Perhaps, but this is what happened. Our organized crime division knew a lot about Rocky and his organization but hadn't been able to put them away. The two enforcers, Mikey and Tony, were well known to them as well. Based on their history, the officers were inclined to believe Gino, but he would still have to answer the firearms charges. They saw an excellent opportunity to offer Gino a deal in exchange for information on Rocky's organization. That would work only, of course, as long as Rocky didn't kill Gino. He was assigned a defense attorney for his arraignment, which took place the next day. Gino must have been nervous, knowing that Rocky would be able to get to him. He knew his life was in danger."

"So, how did he get off?"

"It was all pre-arranged. When Gino appeared in court, his attorney asked for a release on bail, claiming Mr. Barese had no previous record, and the only charge was carrying a 22 without a permit. The judge agreed, and luckily, the amount was low enough for Gino to post the bail for his release. He left jail that morning and decided that he had no choice but to lay low and go underground. From what I heard today, he used that experience later. His task wasn't an easy one. He had to inform on Rocky, but he couldn't face Rocky yet, not after what happened in Caldwell and with Mikey and Tony."

"I get that. But somehow, Gino hung around for another five years without getting killed by Rocky. How do you explain that?"

"That's another story. We kept Gino under wraps for about six months. Mikey went to jail on a trumped-up charge of killing Tony. We put the word out that Mikey had committed the crime. We couldn't risk that Rocky found out the truth because Gino would be useless as an informer if he did. Our OCD did a good job, and no matter how long Mikey denied the charges, the made-up story stuck. We had to wait until after the trial before Gino could surface and seek the graces of his uncle again."

Travis had raised his eyebrows several times during the story. How could the department get away with all that? To think that the DA's office and the lawyers were all in on it seemed so unreal. He was looking for the word illegal, but there was probably no point in bringing that into the conversation after twenty-five years. At first, he was sure that Gino's transgressions had been the motive for the mob to go after him after all. Now that he discovered that Rocky never knew that Gino had killed Tony, the real motivation might still be elusive.

John didn't seem to worry about the whole process of turning a mob figure into a snitch. From earlier comments, he knew that things had not gone smoothly there either. Killing a cop was perhaps the only thing that nobody among the 'city's finest' could forgive and forget. He needed that part of the story and was sure that John was ready to share. He made some notes and looked up at John.

"It's almost lunchtime. Care to join me. I'll let you recommend a place."

"Yeah, you're right, Travis. Let's do that. I'll lock the door, and the file can stay here."

"Yes, because I'll still need to take a look at the info from the OCD later."

"No problem," John said as they left the room. "By the way, I know just the place to go to."

Chapter 32

Tacos For Lunch

John Byrne picked a Mexican place close to the precinct, and they were early enough to get seated right away.

"Best tacos in town," John beamed and put the menu aside.

"Okay with me," Travis said. "Which do you recommend?"

"The pork ones. They're just out of this world," John said while checking the drink list.

"Okay, I'm in," Travis said and thanked the waitress for the water, chips, and salsa.

John ordered a beer and six tacos for both of them. Travis decided to stick to water.

"Before we continue the story," Travis said, "I have a few questions. For instance, O'Grady told me that Gino killed a police officer. You haven't said anything about that."

"I was getting to that; there were a few things that happened before, though."

"Also, I was wondering about an officer named Phinn O'Hara. Do you know him?"

"O'Hara? Hell yes. Not in this precinct, but a guy determined to get people like Gino off the street. Why do you ask?"

"He happens to live in our neighborhood in Durham. I interviewed him a few days ago."

"You're kidding!" John said. "He's your man. You do realize that, right?"

"How so," Travis asked.

"He probably told you the mob almost killed him. He had every reason to kill Gino because he's the one who set him up. I didn't think he could do it, but now that you told me they both moved to your neighborhood, I think he pulled it off."

"I believe he didn't do it. He didn't even know Gino was living there, nor did he recognize him when he saw him."

"I'm sure that's what he told you. I would do the same."

"Really, John?" Travis couldn't believe it. "I'd rather think that you would alert the authorities even after all this time."

"Well, yeah, normally speaking, you may be right," John said. "I'm not so sure about Phinn. I mean, I didn't know him that well. We were all doing the legwork for the detectives, and we had our separate captains. His captain mentioned him once during a multi-precinct briefing about the case against the Fortimare family. He was making some headway, and, of course, Rocky was one of the underbosses.

"Unfortunately, things didn't work out for Phinn, as you probably know," Travis said.

The waitress brought the beer and disappeared. John took a large gulp and smacked his lips. "Yeah, they got to him one day, and I never heard from him again until you just mentioned him."

"Well, he was beaten up pretty badly, so much so that he wasn't able to return to work. Pretty sad, because he was a good cop."

"I'll tell you what, detective Vinder," John said. "Even decent cops don't mind a bit of revenge. I'd talk to Phinn again if I were you."

Travis didn't like where this was going. One officer accusing another of something of which he had no proof didn't sit well with him. Either Phinn was lying, or John didn't know the type of policeman Phinn had been. He briefly tried to figure out what John would gain by making the insinuation. How could one tell whether a cop was on the mob's payroll? He needed to stop this talk. Instead, he'd wanted to concentrate on Gino's story because the next four years in the tale might prove to be more consequential in determining the motive for his murder. A bit in a daydream, he forced his return to the conversation and answered the suggestion.

"You know, I may just do that when I get back to Durham. Anyway..."

John interrupted. "Sure, you find out more in Durham than here from the file."

"But if Phinn has something to do with Gino's murder, he wouldn't have been on the take. Just the opposite," Travis shot back.

John finished his last taco and nodded. He gulped down the rest of his beer and leaned forward. "Let's get back to the precinct.

During their walk, they just talked about the weather and the condition of the sidewalks. To Travis, it appeared that John also didn't want to continue the conversation about Phinn. Perhaps he'd pushed him too far. While reflecting on how he would tackle the afternoon session, he was glad his phone rang.

"Ramón," he said as they arrived at the building, and John held the door for him. "Any news on Jerry?"

"The fingerprints we gathered in the car, the Whitmans home, and the motel came back positive. The guy's name is Marco Conti. He works at an insurance company in Brooklyn. We issued a warrant for his arrest with the department there."

Travis stopped in his tracks. John raised his eyebrows when he heard Travis say: "I was just there this morning. I knew the bastards were involved somehow. I met with a Vinnie Conti. Perhaps his father. What else did you find out about him?"

"There are rumors that he's an enforcer, whatever that means in the insurance business," Ramón said. "If you ask me, he's a hired gun."

"You're right about that. Listen, text me as soon as you hear from the police here. I'll have time to check for myself later," Travis said and hung up.

"What was that all about?" John asked as they took the stairwell to the second-floor office.

"I think we may have our killer. We were quite certain already, but we now have his real name."

"Care to share?" John asked.

"Marco Conti. Does that set off any alarm bells?"

"No, not to me," John said.

On the way to the small room where the file on Gino Barese was waiting for him, he recalled Vinnie's words. Roger Bonelli was retired. Obviously, retirement didn't prohibit him from still having ties with the insurance company. After taking the call from Jim Whitman, Bonelli's first reaction must have been to get in touch with Vinnie, or perhaps directly with Marco Conti. Travis could only imagine that Mr. Whitman had asked for a whole lot more than a nurse. As it turned out, he'd requested a killer to do a job in the Carolina Arbors neighborhood. It just couldn't have been to kill Gino Barese.

The moment John sat down, he took a call on his phone. "Sorry about this," he said, shaking his head. "I got to put out a fire. I'll be back in a few minutes. I'm sure the file will keep you busy."

Chapter 33

Lucille Remembers

Travis leafed through the file as soon as he was alone in the room. He looked for information starting in 1995, but his mind remained preoccupied with the link between the murderer and the insurance company. He began to read the statement Gino gave after his arrest following the shooting of Tony. His phone rang.

"Detective Vinder," he said, turning another page.

"Oh, I'm so glad I could reach you, detective. This is Lucille," he heard the woman say.

"Yes, Lucille. What can I do for you?"

"I'm afraid I left something out of my story this morning. Perhaps it's important."

"Maybe it is," Travis said. "Go ahead."

"Well, when Gino was out of High School, he had a tattoo put on his left arm. I didn't find out later that this was a symbol for a gang. Joe Jr. told me that. It turns out that this U-shaped tattoo with pointed tops was a sign you belonged to the Torellos. I had heard about them a long time ago, but I'm sure all their members graduated into the tougher stuff. My husband never confirmed it, but I had a suspicion that the gang worked the neighborhoods on behalf of the mob in those days."

"Good to know," Travis said, remembering the tattoo he saw on Gino's left wrist. "We had figured as much, and your memory served you well."

"So, this will help you in your current case?" she asked.

"Oh, I'm sure," Travis smiled.

"Good. If I remember anything else, can I call you?"

"Sure," Travis said. "We're trying to wrap our case up in a few days, though. I tell you what. I'll call you once we're done so you won't need to worry about it anymore."

"That'll be fine, detective."

Travis was about to hang up when he suddenly thought of something that struck him as curious. "I do have one more question, if I may. Can you tell me whether your husband ever mentioned your nephew?"

"He never took business home, detective."

"I understand, but Gino was family."

"That's true, but his name never came up."

"Did you see Gino after 1995?"

"I believe once, at Joe Sr.'s funeral. He sat in the back of the church. I don't believe he talked to either his cousins or me. During the four years leading up to 9/11, we never saw him or heard of him again. I don't think there was a family service after he was officially declared dead. I never heard from Annamarie, so..."

"I see. Well, that's all for now. Thanks for your help."

"You're welcome," Lucille said and hung up the phone.

Travis jotted down 1997 and the word funeral. Rocky had been no threat to Gino after that, but with Joe Jr. in the slammer,

Vinnie was still a cousin to be reckoned with. To this day, as it turned out.

Chapter 34

The Dossier

John returned when Travis started to read about conversations between Gino as an informer and a detective. There was a reference to the troubles in Caldwell.

"Want some coffee?" John asked.

"No, thanks," Travis said. "I've just found something about the report on the killing at a Laundromat. What can you tell me about that?"

John pulled his chair closer to the table. "That happened about two years after the trial of Mikey. By then, Gino was working for his uncle again and acting as an informant to us. Well, not to me, but for the detective on Rocky's case."

"I see," Travis said. "What kind of information did he provide the detective with."

"You can read about that in the dossier, but in a nutshell, I can tell you that it was mostly about the movement of stolen goods or contraband. I heard that they smuggled thousands of cigarette sleeves out of North Carolina and sold them in New York. The profits were huge."

"Was the information accurate, and what did the detective do with it?" Travis asked.

"There never was any proof of Rocky's direct involvement, and even if there was a hint of it, nothing ever stuck as far as an arrest was concerned."

"So why did the department hold on to Gino?"

"You know, waiting for the big break."

"Which never came."

"No, it didn't. Quite the opposite, you see."

"Tell me," Travis said, pushing the file a bit further in front of him.

"Well, you can imagine that Gino wasn't particularly safe in Rocky's presence. We knew that Mikey kept yelling from his jail cell that he was innocent and that it had been Gino who killed Tony. Rocky had reason to believe his lieutenant, given the circumstances in which they had left the house. Gino had to be killed, and Rocky knew that Mikey would never let Gino escape. Something happened, but as I said, the case at trial was ironclad, so to speak."

"Did Gino ever say anything about Rocky not trusting him again?"

"Oh, he did all the time."

"And how did the detective respond to that?" Travis asked.

"He told Gino that as long as he appeared to do the work for his uncle, the trust would be re-established. The police protected informants, so he shouldn't be so worried."

"Until?"

"Indeed. Gino became more and more involved, at one point taking Mikey's place in the organization. That meant that violence was back on the table. That eventually led to the killing of one of ours at the Laundromat."

"Tell me what happened."

"Gino had been disappointed at the insurance proceeds that were to be paid by the owner of the place. After several threats, the man had asked for some real police protection. There was a rumor that Rocky was going to show up. It was a perfect setup for us as we would catch Rocky in his racketeering crime. An undercover cop spent his time at the store."

"Why did they think Rocky would show up?"

"Gino told us that his uncle was getting very impatient and had made references to taking the matter into his own hands. Hence, the undercover operation."

"But Rocky never showed up."

"Correct. On that fateful day, Gino and another thug showed up just before the manager left. They hustled the man to the back office, and our undercover man was growing anxious, hearing screams of pain from that area. He busted in just as Gino was wielding a gun, using it as a hammer on the poor man's skull. Seeing our guy go for a weapon, Gino didn't hesitate and fired a shot right away. It was just one single shot that killed a cop. Gino and his buddy fled the store, and the manager identified them from photos. Gino was now wanted and no longer an informant."

"So what happened to him. Was he ever arrested?"

"No. Gino went underground. We believe that killing a cop put him in good graces with Rocky but wanted by the law. In the grand scheme of things, Gino was a liability."

"So, that's the last you guys heard of Gino Barese."

"Not really. About a year later, the New York Times ran an exposé on the mafia's practices illustrated with a pretty accurate and detailed organizational chart. Both Mikey and Gino featured in the story together with the other players you already know. As a result of that article, someone at the DA's office started talking. It was the end of Gino's mob career. A witness divulged that something about Mikey's case smelled rotten in the state of Denmark. There was a new trial a year later, and Micky was re-sentenced to a much lesser charge. Having done enough time, he was released. You can imagine that Rocky wanted Gino Barese's hide."

"I guess so. But I gather, Rocky never found Gino."

"Neither did we. Rocky died of cancer, and Gino went deep. For all we knew, he'd left the country. The name never came up until a few years later. We couldn't believe it when we found out. He'd been under our noses the whole time."

"And then the file was closed."

"Indeed. So, we never got the conviction for killing one of our own, but I'm going to guess that it was someone working for the mob that finally got Barese. If you're looking for a motive, you've got it now."

"Yes and no," Travis said. "You see, how did the mob know that Gino was alive and where he was living."

"Beats me."

"Would it surprise you when I said that he lived under an assumed name in Jersey City? That he lived there for almost twenty years?"

"I had no clue," John said, shaking his head.

"I realize it's like a needle in a haystack, but I'm surprised that no-one ever recognized him there. It took a move to North Carolina to get him recognized by three people right away."

"It's just pure luck, I think," John said.

"Not necessarily so. I do know that there is every reason to believe that the mob, or their associates, knew that Gino was still alive after 9/11. That leaves the question, who else might have known, and are they the ones that tipped off the mob?"

"Not sure what you're getting at, detective."

"What if it was someone in your department who happened to find out where he moved to and informed members of the Fortimare family to do the dirty work?"

"Is that a guess?" John asked.

"Sure it is, but it could've happened that way," Travis said. "I do have a question. Besides you, who here at the precinct knows about the Gino Barese case file?"

"A bunch of guys, of course. Most are retired, as you can imagine. You already visited detective O'Grady."

"Does anyone else come to mind?"

John reflected for a few moments. His answers had grown terse, and his tone was highly defensive. Travis couldn't let his impromptu questioning go. If only he could find a link between the police department and the insurance company. If it were in the form of a current or ex-officer, that would solidify his thinking at the moment. Accusing John of something at this point made no sense, of course. He repeated his question in part. "Anyone?"

"No, I wouldn't know where to begin. It would be almost like accusing someone. That would be wrong," John answered, oblivious that this was precisely what he'd done during lunch.

"Right. I'm almost done here. I'm going to read the rest of your written report and check a few of the documents. I should finish that in about an hour. There's no need for you to hang around."

John sighed. "Okay. I got some loose ends on my desk anyway. I'll be back later."

After John left, Travis continued reading the summary at the point where the writer assumed that Rocky targeted Gino for the murder of Tony. Rocky's death was never mentioned as most of the story concentrated on many other criminal infractions by

Gino. Then came the moment in the report when the police confirmed the death of Gino Barese in the South Tower. Travis read this last page carefully.

Gino Barese was last seen entering the South Tower on September 11, 2001. He wore a light raincoat, no hat, and no briefcase or bag. He was seen stubbing out a cigarette near the left entrance. None of the subsequent video recordings showed him leaving the building. It was established in court that Mr. Barese had an appointment with a company with offices at the Tower. However, a police report did indicate that a man with similar features left the building shortly after 9 AM. Even though the man's face was not recognized, most of the company employees left the building, and it was likely that Mr. Barese equally walked away. Based on this report, a Surrogate's Court judge denied Mrs. Angie Barese's petition to have him declared a victim of the attacks. However, on January 31, 2003, a New York State appeals court overturned the lower-court ruling. It declared that he had been a victim of the attacks, officially making him the 2,721st victim of the Twin Towers' collapse. The plaintiff in the case was represented by Mr. James Whitman, Esq.

Chapter 35

Unidentified Victims

Travis looked at his smartphone. He had two hours before heading for the airport to catch his returning flight to Raleigh. John had returned briefly to the room and collected the file on Gino Barese. Before they said goodbye, Travis had requested to see the New York Chief of Police. John arranged with a simple call, and Travis waited in the same room.

Things started to connect, and he had a pretty good idea about the people he now had to keep an eye on. Last, he added John to the list. The Conti's were clearly on his mind, but so was Mr. Whitman. He was sure that the order of events might reveal a significant clue in the murder of Gino. Jim Whitman's additional link to Gino Barese's case by representing the family was puzzling at best. Marco Conti rented a car and checked into a motel under the name Jerry Darcay. That was about two months ago. Whitman must have known Carlo as Gino, but there was no proof he ever ran into him at the Arbors, nor did he kill him given his physical condition. However, someone at the insurance company, most likely Vinnie, sent Marco with a purpose. The latter killed the man known as Carlo. It stood to reason that Marco knew that Carlo was actually Gino. That information could not have come from Jim Whitman. Instead, it must have been Vinnie who told him, figuring that he knew that Gino never died at the towers. If Whitman was a lawyer for Bonelli at the insurance company, why did he declare that Gino had perished on 9/11? Another question yet unanswered was why Marco got to Carolina Arbors way before Gino moved there? Something was missing, and Travis was hoping to get some cooperation from the Chief of Police.

The door opened swiftly, and Chief of Police Terrance Johnson stood in the door opening. Behind him appeared the tall figure of ex-detective Paddy O'Grady. Surprised, Travis shook the Chief of Police's hand and briefly nodded at Paddy. "Wow, the full Monty, heh?"

"Yes, Detective Vinder," Terrance said and sat down, showing a chair to Paddy. "Detective O'Grady here called me a little while ago, and what he told me about your investigation raised some questions."

"Join the crowd," Travis said, sitting down as well. "I've got some ideas, but not all the answers."

"In that case, let's see whether you can answer our questions, and we can answer your questions."

"Fair enough," Travis said. "You're obviously aware that Gino Barese took on another identity after 9/11 and became Carlo Messina. I figured out that some in the mob knew that. I also figured that someone in law enforcement knew. But who?"

"That's why I'm here," Paddy said. "It didn't hit me until you left earlier this morning, but I was wondering the same thing."

Chief of Police Johnson took over. "Yes, Paddy called me while you were out to lunch with John, and I asked him who might have known. We have to go back more than twenty years to answer that question."

"I'm listening," Travis said.

"When I told you about the undercover officer killed by Gino, I'd forgotten that Joe Malinski had been his partner on the beat years ago. I assume Joe didn't tell you that. He later was assigned to a different precinct, where he became a detective

"I see," Travis said, "But, then again, I never told Joe about Gino simply because I didn't know about him. I mentioned Carlo, of course."

"I get that," Johnson said. "You probably didn't know that Phinn O'Hara was assigned to the task force investigating Joe Conti Sr., known as Rocky."

"So Joe knew Phinn?" Travis asked, sitting up.

"No, he didn't," Paddy answered. "You see, Joe was at a different precinct. Besides, he didn't become a detective until Phinn left the force after the mob had beaten him severely. I honestly think they never met."

"So, what is significant about all this?"

"We believe that one of the two may have been a target of the mob," the Chief of Police said.

"What?"

"Hear me out," Johnson said. "Phinn had built a strong case linking the insurance company of Bonelli & Partners to the Fortimare family. The authorities checked out the company and the books, but the report cited no evidence. Yet that's why the mob targeted O'Hara. The fact that we couldn't prove it didn't mean that link didn't exist."

"So, that would explain him being a target, but how about Joe Malinski?"

"As a detective, he built a stronger case against Rocky. Unfortunately, Vinnie's father died before the charges stuck. Joe Jr. may have found out about Malinski and put a hit on him. Even from jail, he made all sorts of threats."

"You'll excuse me for taking all this with a grain of salt," Travis said, leaning back on his chair. "What you're insinuating is that Malinski, O'Hara, and Gino are all connected somehow and that all three moved at different times to one single neighborhood in North Carolina? I find that hard to believe."

"In a way, that's exactly what happened."

Travis looked at Paddy. "What do you think? You were a detective on the case as well, right?"

"Yes and no. I spent my time on the bigger picture with the Fortimare bosses."

Travis stared at the Chief of Police. "So, the mob may have had three targets, all living within one square mile of each other?"

"It appears so, but only one target didn't survive."

"I believe that whoever had it out for them didn't know about O'Hara and Malinski living there."

"So, that is just a coincidence?"

"Must be," Johnson said. "However, we do have some questions and wondered whether you had resolved them."

"What do you want to know?"

"Who set Gino up?"

"Someone who's involved with the mob and recognized Carlo as Gino, or someone who belonged to the precinct."

"Why would you link the precinct to Gino's murder?"

"Well, for one, John alluded to it. You must be aware that law enforcement was after Gino as well."

"At one time, yes, perhaps," Johnson said. "A year and a half after 9/11, that case was closed."

"Oh, I realize that," Travis said. "Closed by John. Did you ever read his final report, chief?"

"I glanced it over, yes."

"Would it surprise you if I told you that John alluded to Phinn O'Hara as possibly being the one who told the mob about Gino's improbable resurrection as Carlo Messina? That fact alone would've caused the mob to act?"

"Now, why would he do that?"

"That's what I wondered about," Travis said. "I've talked with Phinn, and nothing appears to indicate anything about revenge about what the mob did to him. He didn't even recognize Gino."

"And your conclusion?"

"John took a stab in the dark. It was the wrong stab. Phinn's not involved."

"Assuming you're right," Paddy said. "How did the killer, whoever he is, find Gino?"

"I'm working on that," Travis answered. "I have some other links that we need to firm up. We've identified the killer. He's Marco Conti, most likely the son of Vinnie Conti, who went by the name of Jerry Darcay."

"Is he still in North Carolina?"

"We believe he came back here, and we've already sent a multi-state warrant for his arrest. You should have gotten that by now."

"I hope we did."

"You may as well go after Vinnie Conti is well. He runs Bonelli & Partners. You have a charge that may stick for a change. Here's the address on Flatbush in Brooklyn," Travis said, pushing a piece of paper to the police chief.

"We're on it," Johnson said. "So this Marco guy followed Gino to North Carolina and killed him there?"

"Not quite. Here's the puzzle. Marco was already in the neighborhood weeks before Gino showed up."

"Then the mob knew Gino's whereabouts, assumed name and his plans, way before the move."

"I don't believe so," Travis said. "I think our answer lies in North Carolina in the neighborhood where everything culminated in the killing of Gino. I tend to believe that the mob didn't know about Gino until he actually moved there."

"Are you telling us that it is either Malinski or O'Hara after all?"

"No, I'm not. I think it's the person who brought in Marco to begin with."

"And you know who that is?" Paddy asked.

"I do. His name is Jim Whitman. He had a stroke and needed nursing assistance in his home. According to his wife, he's the one who called Roger Bonelli."

"Really? That's interesting. This goon has been under investigation for years, even after his retirement. What's the link?"

"I'm surprised you're asking me. Roger founded the insurance company, and I already told you that Vinnie works there."

"But that doesn't link them to Gino Barese, who for all practical purposes had died in the towers," the chief said.

"Ah, but therein lies the misdirection," Travis said. "I believe that Vinnie and many of the employees who worked at their office in the South Tower made it out. Rest assured that they all knew that Gino made it out as well."

"If that's the case, we're looking at an opportunistic moment for murder because someone recognized Carlo as Gino."

"That's correct," Travis said. "So, as soon as I get back to North Carolina, I'll determine two things: why did Mr. Whitman call Roger Bonelli, and who recognized Gino."

"And, you'll let us know," the chief said.

"Of course, I'll wrap this up from my end by tomorrow. I trust you guys get the killer, and most likely, we can wrap this up soon."

"I agree, and good work, detective," Chief Johnson said. "We'll get not only the murderer, but also that insurance outfit, and if we can make it stick, Roger Bonelli."

"That would end some of your open cases," Travis said, getting up.

"I agree," Paddy said. "Listen, can I take you to the airport?"

"If you don't mind," Travis said. "I do have plenty of time."

"Oh, no, you don't," Paddy smiled. "You have no idea about traffic at this time of the day."

Travis put away his notebook and shook hands with the Chief of Police. He didn't see John again as he left the precinct with Paddy.

Chapter 36

Catching A Flight

The drive to Newark Airport proved indeed to be a long haul with jammed traffic everywhere. The stop-and-go trip was made bearable only because of the conversation between the two detectives.

"I appreciate the lift," Travis had started.

"Oh, glad to do it," Paddy said. "I had some questions for you, just out of curiosity, you know, nothing that was important to the chief."

"I get it," Travis said, a little distracted. He was reading a text from Ramón on his phone. There had been an attempt to take in Marco Conti, but he eluded the officers minutes before the bust. Ramón had added 'as if he knew they were coming.' He continued: "Once we get the murderer, we'll learn a lot more."

"That's what I wanted to talk about," Paddy said.

"Okay, I'm listening," Travis said, turning to the driver.

"I don't know this Marco guy, but I know all about his dad, Vinnie, if we believe it is the son. I think your visit this morning alerted him enough to get his kid to go below the radar. He'll be hard to find."

"Then a look into tying Marco to the office and bringing in Vinnie as an accessory wouldn't be that hard, right?"

"I'm sure Johnson's on it. When I was still on the case, we had several people on that insurance outfit. At one time, their only policies were the unwritten contracts to collect from store owners. When that came under scrutiny, the employees became licensed insurance agents, and they were actually starting to sell auto and homeowners insurance. It became harder and harder to make our prepared charges stick. Their link to the Fortimare family likewise was hard to prove. Vinnie's a smart guy. I didn't think that murder was on his to-do list, but obviously, his dad's desire for revenge for Tony's killing may have changed his ways. Finding Gino, no matter how or who ratted on him, made this revenge irresistible."

"I agree. I believe it solidifies the main motive. Depending on who ratted on Gino as you offered as a possibility, there may have been a second underlying motive."

"You mean someone on the force had the mob do the dirty work as a revenge for the killing of the undercover officer."

"Exactly. I'm glad you picked up on that during our talk with Johnson. I wonder how he will deal with that."

"Is it fair to state that you believe that someone with a link to the mob or Vinnie's office may have been a retired law enforcement person who lives in your neighborhood?"

"It's a possibility. However, I don't think it points to the obvious suspects or suspects."

"How do you mean?" Paddy asked.

"Phinn O'Hara is too obvious, and I believe his statement. He lied to me once but felt so guilty that he set that straight in no time. I'm not even sure he knew who beat him or had beaten him up. On the other hand, there's retired detective Malinski."

"Joe? I'm not sure. He would have informed either the local authorities or the people in New York."

"So, that leaves only one person with a link to the city and the crime family: Jim Whitman."

"You didn't tell us much about him. How did he come to call the insurance company again?"

"I only know that he knew Roger. At the time, I had no idea who that was. Now, Whitman was a lawyer who cleaned up things for Bonelli, either personally or for the firm. It was also Whitman who was the lawyer for the Barese family who wanted him declared dead. You can count on the fact that I'll be visiting with Mr. Whitman again tomorrow."

"I think he's indeed the key to solving this."

"I agree."

Paddy opened his window and yelled something at the driver of a car next to him. The slow drive was getting on his nerves. Paddy calmed down and seemed happier when traffic picked up. However, it remained quiet for a while as if they had said all there was to say.

Nearing the airport, Paddy broke the silence. "United?"

"Yes, thanks."

"What time are you getting home?"

"If we take off on time, I should be home by nine."

"Sorry about the timing. You'll be missing dinner," Paddy said as he slowly drove to the terminal.

"No worries, my wife will have something ready to warm up," Travis said. "Anyway, thanks for the ride and the conversation. There's one thing, though, that puzzled me a bit this afternoon?"

"Oh, what's that?" Paddy asked.

"The fact that you showed up with the Chief of Police."

"Oh, that," Paddy said, turning toward the curb. "After we talked, I had called him and told him all about the Gino Barese file and case. He wasn't familiar with the dossier, so I decided to go in and give him some background. These days there's little to do in the way of mob investigations. It's more street crime and white-collar crime."

"I see," Travis said. "Okay, we're here. Thanks again, and I'll be in touch."

Travis slammed the door shut after he retrieved his small bag from the rear seat. He entered the terminal and made his call to Ramón. By morning, Travis wanted to know everything about Mr. and Mrs. Whitman before going out there as his first call of the day.

Chapter 37

A Club Revisited

Hungry and ready to get home, Travis headed for the parking lot at RDU Airport. Seeing a police SUV sitting in front of his car got his attention. Clearly, Ramón had a story to tell.

"Hi, Ramón," he said as the officer got out of his car.

"Travis," Ramón nodded briefly. "Got some things on our Mr. Whitman."

"I figured. What did you find?" Travis asked as he unlocked his car and put his overnight bag on the passenger seat.

"It took a bit of digging, mostly by Julia. Jim Whitman was a defense attorney."

"I know. In New York, right?"

"Delaware. At least his office was located there."

"He did have clients in New York."

"I know what you're going for, but we couldn't find any case he defended in any borough. However, he did plenty of work in Delaware and New Jersey."

"Mafia cases?"

"Some, but not exclusive."

"I texted you all the names we discussed in New York yesterday. He did work for Bonelli and the Barese family. Anything come up?"

"Yes, and that's why I'm here. I think we may want to visit Mr. Whitman tonight."

Travis felt a sudden pang in his stomach, thinking about a dinner postponed. "What did you discover?"

"You mentioned a Mikey Freese, and it turns out he has a brother named Hal. This fellow lives in Creedmoor, not too far from here."

"And?"

"Jim Whitman represented him in a criminal case twenty-three years ago."

"So, there's a link between this Hal character, Bonelli & Partners and Whitman. Whitman said he called Bonelli, so we already know about that link."

"Perhaps it was Hal Freese who recognized Gino Barese and told Whitman about it. Whitman called for help, and that guy Vinnie you mentioned was alerted. He could be the one who sent Marco down here to take care of Gino. What do you think?"

"Good reasoning, Ramón. There's one problem with that. Remember that Jerry, aka Marco Conti, arrived here at least seven weeks ago, before Gino ever set foot at the Arbors."

"Crap, you're right, of course. This Hal guy nor Mr. Whitman could've foreseen Carlo, I mean Gino, moving from Jersey. Unless someone did find out ahead of time."

"Which I doubt," Travis concluded the thought. "This doesn't mean that Hal Freese isn't involved in this case."

"So, I expect you're going to question Mr. Whitman to get to the bottom of this?"

"Let's both go. I'll call Maureen about being very late for dinner."

"Aha, I took care of that," Travis smiled as he reached into his car. He handed Travis a large Jersey Mike's bag. "You're favorite club sandwich. I got you a lemonade as well."

"Hey, now that's perfect," Travis said. "Another Jersey connection. That's all we need. On the way, let Mr. Whitman know that we'll be there in ten minutes."

Chapter 38

The Link

Mrs. Whitman opened the front door and stared at Travis and Ramón. She appeared defiant, clenching her left fist on her hip, her greeting proving she wasn't amused. "Do you know what time it is? We'd already retired for the day, and Jimmy was sound asleep when you called. What's so important?"

"I have some urgent questions in the case we're working on," Travis answered. "Rather than having you picked up and brought to the station, I figured this visit is more for your convenience."

"Hah! We can't possibly help you any further in your case," she snarled.

"Oh, yes, you can. May we come in?" Travis asked.

Mrs. Whitman opened the door a bit wider. "Now, do you need my husband for this?"

"Not if you can answer our questions," Travis said.

"You could've asked me on the phone," she said.

"As I said," Travis said a little firmer than he had intended, "We could have done this at the station, which would be more inconvenient for your husband."

Mrs. Whitman rubbed her left arm and sat down in a nearby chair. "What do you want to know?"

Travis remained standing. "During my last visit, you told me that your husband called a fellow in New York. Following the call, Jerry came down to help him out after his stroke. Did Jim make that call, or did you make it?"

"I dialed for him, and he talked with Mr. Bonelli."

"And how did you or your husband know Mr. Bonelli?"

"You must know, my husband was a defense lawyer, and during a case, he met him once. I remembered that case paying a lot of our bills. At the time, Roger told us not to hesitate to call him if we ever needed him. You see, Jim got an acquittal for his client."

"And why did you call him for this specialized help?"

"We didn't get anywhere with our own secondary insurance company, and it looked like a good call."

"I see," Travis said and paused. He felt that there was more to the story since the fellow dispatched turned out to be a killer. There must have been a reason to send that kind of criminal, and though it might have nothing to do with Gino's murder, something was missing. In effect, saying *I see* wasn't right. "Now, Mrs. Whitman, how did you know that the insurance company had a nurse like Jerry available. It seems to be an expensive undertaking. The travel for Jerry, his stay at a motel, his per diem, and his fees all add up. I believe you said you paid him weekly. Do you have any proof of payment?"

Mrs. Whitman hesitated. "Did I say that? I don't recall saying we paid him by check. You see, we paid him in cash if you must know."

"As you may gather by now, we suspect Jerry's involvement in the incident at Piedmont Hall. Did you know he might have ulterior motives to come here?"

"Of course not, detective."

"How good was he as a nurse?"

"We've never had a person like this, but he took good care of Jim and seemed to know what he was doing. I believe you already know that."

"I just wanted confirmation at this point," Travis said as he took a few steps toward the ground floor master bedroom. "I believe I need to speak to your husband."

Mrs. Whitman got up reluctantly and opened the bedroom door. Jim sat up in bed and coughed lightly as Travis and Ramón entered. He lifted his hand to say hello.

"Mr. Whitman, we talked to your wife about your call to Roger Bonelli. Did you talk to him or someone else?"

Mr. Whitman cleared his throat. "I talked to him."

"Do you have the number you called?"

Jim looked at his wife without saying a word. The woman went to a dresser, pulled it open, and took out a business card. She handed it to Travis.

The card had the same logo he'd seen in the lobby of the insurance company he visited the day before. The name below the logo showed Ruggieri Bonelli. There was a single telephone number. "And you called this number?"

"Yes. I asked for him. A man transferred me to Roger's mobile phone."

"Did you ask him whether he still worked at his insurance company?"

"I saw no reason to," Jim said.

"Mr. Bonelli must have owed you quite a bit to send you a private nurse."

"That's the way he felt, I guess."

"Did you speak to anyone else at his company?"

"I did because he's retired, but not until the next day when someone called us back."

"And what else did you talk to Mr. Bonelli about?"

"Oh, many things. I told him where we lived now and that I retired. I remember telling him that many Yankees had moved here."

"Did you tell him about the Men's Dinner Club you belonged to?"

Mr. Whitman reflected for a moment. "As a matter of fact, I did. I told him I hated to leave that club because I have some good friends there."

Travis looked at Ramón, and it remained quiet for a few moments. Ramón seemed to shrug his shoulders. Travis redirected his eyes on Mr. Whitman. "did you happen to mention some of the people in the club?"

"Why would I do that?"

"How about names?"

"I remember telling him about the fact that I was in safe company because two of them were ex-cops."

"Right," Travis said. "Tell me about the call you got."

"That was the next day, as I said," Mr. Whitman said. "My wife took the call, and the man wanted to talk to me."

"Tell me a little about how that conversation went."

"The guy's name was Conti or something. He said he was an associate of Mr. Bonelli. He said he had good news for us. He was going to send a nurse down for about a month or so at little cost to us."

"Did this Conti person ask about your friends in the club?"

"He might have, I don't remember," Mr. Whitman said and suddenly seemed tired as he rested his head on his propped up pillow.

"Did he mention a name?"

"He said that he heard from Roger that one was called O'Hara. All he asked me was whether he was from Brooklyn."

"And what did you answer?"

"I told him that I thought so but wasn't sure."

Ramón coughed lightly, drawing the attention of Travis. The officer made a slight gesture with his hand slicing across his throat. Travis was confused. Did Ramón refer to the slashing of the victim, or did he want the interrogation to stop? He thought to let Ramón handle it.

"Officer, did you have any questions for the Whitmans at this point?" Travis asked.

"Oh, no, detective," Ramón said. "I think we have all we need."

"Okay, then," Travis said. He looked at the elderly couple. "I can't promise we won't need to talk to you again, but it may be a few days. And yes, if possible, I'll do it over the phone."

"That would be a good idea," Mrs. Whitman said as she left the bedroom and let them out.

Standing by Travis' car, Ramón shook his head. "I never saw that coming, did you?"

"You mean O'Hara?"

"Exactly. Phinn was the target. From what you told me about Conti and having heard what O'Hara told us, it's as simple as putting two and two together."

"I almost missed that," Travis said. He rubbed his eyes. "It's been a long day. For a minute there, I thought that we needed to talk about the slashing, but then it finally dawned on me. Anyway, O'Hara was unfinished business for the Fortimare family. Marco Conti was sent to take care of that."

"For some reason, that didn't work out."

"If we could get our hands on the killer, we may find out two things. Why he didn't kill O'Hara and why he killed Gino."

"Gino was a much more valuable target for a revenge killing. Jerry's, sorry, Marco Conti's assignment must have switched once his boss discovered that Gino had moved to Carolina Arbors."

"I'm guessing that Marco didn't know Gino given the age difference. I have a hunch that Mikey's brother Hal either knew Gino or, at a minimum, heard about him. Even if he didn't work for Rocky, he worked with the mob."

"So, we're heading for Creedmoor?"

"Not at this point. I'm calling it a day. Stay alert for any news about Marco. When they pick him up in New York, we'll need to arrange the extradition."

"How does that work, and how long does it take?"

"If he fights the extradition through a writ of habeas corpus, we need our governor's office to make a case to the New York governor's office. We would have to wait for the result of the extradition hearing. That may take a month or longer."

"But, it just delays justice, right?"

"Indeed. First, let's see if our colleagues in New York can get Marco. All states should have been alerted by now."

Chapter 39

The Uber Driver

Hal Freese was waiting in the holding lot at RDU airport. An earlier ride from Creedmoor with a customer had been good. He checked the app on his phone and saw that he'd gotten a ten dollar tip. Counting about twelve cars in front of him, he figured he would catch another ride out soon. Hopefully, it wouldn't be a short ride like a couple of weeks ago when he rode out to that retirement community called Carolina Arbors. He dropped his ride off near a recently built home. He'd remained parked there, wavering between heading back for the airport right away or waiting for a ride from the neighborhood.

He decided to wait for about ten minutes. He stared at the small narrow house standing almost alone on the street with only one neighbor on the side and a tall stand of trees left on the other side where the ground had been too narrow to carve out a lot. It looked like an afterthought perched on the tiny area where the building company had squeezed in one more home before pulling out of the neighborhood.

Moments later, a gray Honda pulled into the driveway, stopped for a minute while the garage door opened, and pulled in. He hadn't paid much attention to the man who waved a small moving truck toward the house. Hal had sat up straight the moment he saw someone helping the two movers. His heart skipped more than just one beat, and he couldn't believe his eyes. It couldn't be! Was this Gino Barese? He grabbed his phone, alerted his old boss, and sent the pictures he'd taken.

That was then. Tomorrow, Hal would see his meager savings account increase tenfold. He was tempted to go back to the neighborhood and determine whether there was a rumor mill about the investigation. He was told not to go there unless he had a rider there. His app pinged, and he was up next. The rider's name appeared as Ramón.

Ramón had done his best work late the night before. Hal Freese was easy to track down, and having nothing else to do, Ramón drove over to the listed address. He considered it pure luck to see a white Toyota Camry sitting in front of the doublewide. A quick run of the license plates confirmed the owner as Hal Freese. The Uber sticker had sent him on to a clever ruse. Now waiting at the airport, he had called in his arrangement with the Uber office. If everything worked out, Hal should be on his way to pick him up.

Travis was waiting in the office, having gotten a text from Ramón that they should be there in about twenty minutes. Travis knew that the missing link was being presented on a platter by Ramón. Full cooperation would confirm how the murder of Gino became set in motion.

Ramón had listed the department's address for the Uber ride. Hal was surprised to see a police officer get into his car, and

Ramón told him to drive to the location given. Arriving at the station, Hal was set to leave as soon as Ramón got out. He was surprised when the officer put his hand on his arm.

"Hal, thanks for the ride, but you need to come in with me," Ramón said.

"Me? What the hell! I didn't violate any traffic laws."

"No, you didn't," Ramón said. "There's a detective Vinder that has a few questions for you?"

"You're kidding me, right?" Hal protested. "You tricked me into coming to the police station."

"I guess I did," Ramón admitted. "This won't take long, I'm sure. You can leave your car here, and you'll be on your way soon."

"I don't like this. I haven't done anything wrong, officer," Hal whined.

"I didn't say you did," Ramón smiled. "We're working on a case, and we believe you may have seen something that can help us."

"So, I'm not in trouble?"

"Nope," Ramón said. "Hand me your keys. The sooner we get in, the sooner you can leave."

Hal handed over his keys and got out of the car. Ramón showed him to one of the interrogation rooms where Travis was waiting.

"Hal Freese?" Travis asked, making sure he'd cross all his t's during this recorded questioning.

"Yes, sir," Hal responded.

"Detective Travis Vinder. Have a seat. I gather Officer Acosta introduced himself to you?"

"Yes, sir."

"Good. We've brought you in to clear some things up in the case of the murder of Carlo Messina."

"Do I know that person?" Hal shot back.

"You know him by his original name, Gino Barese."

"So?"

"As an Uber driver, I'm sure you frequent the Carolina Arbors neighborhood, right?"

"I do give rides there."

"Good, so I can imagine your surprise when you ran into Gino, right?"

"Is that where he lived now."

"So, you knew he was alive."

Hal realized his mistake. "Just a guess."

"I'm going to take that as affirmative," Travis said. "Knowing he was alive but not knowing where, you too were on the lookout for Tony's killer, weren't you?"

"Tony?" Hal asked. "I'm not sure what you're talking about."

"Well, perhaps you forgot the mob lieutenant, but you do remember your brother, Mikey, right?"

"All of this is New York stuff. I have nothing to do with this."

"You do remember that your brother was charged in the murder of Tony?"

"Oh, that Tony. That was a long time ago. Still, that case belongs to the NY police."

"You would like to think that, but that case is now closed, given that not your brother, but Gino was the killer."

"If that case is closed, why am I here?"

"You know a Mr. James Whitman?"

Hal hesitated briefly. "Yes. He once successfully defended me in a case."

"Are you aware he too lives at Carolina Arbors?"

"I didn't know that."

"Are you sure? I mean, he did such a great job in your case that the mob owed him. You would do anything for him, right?"

"I might, depending on what it was. I haven't spoken to my contact in over fifteen years."

"Noted," Travis said. "Now, I'm not saying you told Mr. Whitman about Gino, but why did you tell Mr. Conti in New York?"

"Who said I did. I haven't been in the city for years."

"I visited with Mr. Conti yesterday and had a long talk with him. You might as well come clean."

The hesitation lasted longer this time as Hal tapped his fingers on the table, looking at Ramón and then at Travis. "What did he tell you?"

"I found him a reasonable man," Travis replied. "I'm, however, more interested in your version of what happened."

Hal sat back and leaned back. "What do you want to know?"

"Start by telling us what happened after you spotted Gino."

"I checked on his home a few more times after moving day. He lived quietly at the end of the street. The shades in the windows were down all the time, and you had to look carefully to make out the bluish glow of the TV that played far into the night, every night."

"So, you staked out his place."

"Before and after my shifts. I needed to make sure that the man I saw was indeed Gino. Mr. Conti told me he had to be absolutely sure. One day Gino came out. He had no idea I followed him. He drove to the Kroger store on Miami Boulevard, all the way on Highway 70 for his groceries. I found that he did all his business in Durham instead of shopping at the nearby stores. For once, he seemed not to be careful like he had been before. I followed him into the store. With a little luck, I would hear him talk because I never forgot the raspy, guttural sound. It was easy to catch up with him in the checkout line because he most likely would not recognize me as I only saw him in court during my brother's case. At that time, I always wore shades and sported a mustache. I managed to get out of the store before he did and took several close-ups. His left wrist was exposed while carrying his bags, and the Torellos tattoo was clearly visible."

"So, you confirmed your sighting and pictures with Mr. Conti, right?"

"I did."

"Do you know either a Jerry Darcay or Marco Conti?"

"I've heard of Marco but never met him. How's he involved?"

"Do you know what he does for a living?"

"Not really. I thought Marco worked for the insurance company, no?"

"In a way," Travis said. "Now, when you divulged the whereabouts of Gino Barese to Mr. Conti, what did you think was going to happen?"

"Uh, I don't know. I guess it was just proof of what a lot in the company knew."

"And that is?"

"That he was indeed alive, hiding all this time, never bothering even to change his looks. Anyone else in his situation would have had some surgery done; you know what I'm saying? That's just a sloppy attitude."

"He did change his name, assuming someone else's identity," Travis volunteered. "But you must have known that he was wanted. People were looking for him. You said so yourself."

"I guess I did."

"So, you also must have known what those people would do to Gino, once they got to him."

"I'm sure they weren't going to send him a birthday card."

"Not funny, Hal. How about sending someone out to kill him?"

"I've got nothing to do with that. I wasn't involved."

"Yes, you were. You admitted letting people know where they could get their hands on him, knowing very well that it would lead to his demise."

"I couldn't have known for sure."

"And your case handled by Mr. Whitman shows that you know all of this too well. As far as I can tell, you're an accessory in the murder of Mr. Barese," Travis said. "I'm going to let the DA office weigh in on this."

"Wait, no!" Hal said. "I honestly didn't know what they were going to do. You can't arrest me."

"We're just holding you here until the Assistant DA gets here."

"Wait. If I tell you more, can you just let this go?"

"I'd like to see what else you have for me, but the decision on the charges is up to the DA's office. Meanwhile, what else can you tell me?"

"What do you want to know?"

"Did you follow Mr. Barese anywhere else?"

"I did. One morning, he walked into that big central building over there. That's where I overheard a conversation about a men's club. I checked at the front desk, and they told me what it was. But I never saw him again."

"And you reported this to Mr. Conti?"

"I did."

"What else?"

"I was hoping to spot him again in that building, but he didn't show. A week later, I walked up to the front desk to ask about Gino, but they didn't know anyone by that name in their neighborhood. That's when I saw this announcement on their activities screen about the Men's Dinner Club meeting."

"And you called that in?"

"I did. I had no choice. I owed Mr. Conti for getting the legal help I needed."

"Good to know," Travis said. "And you're sure you never met a Jerry Darcay?"

"Nope. That's all, detective. I swear. Can I go now?" Hal pleaded.

"All I can do is talk to the Assistant DA," Travis said as he stood up and turned to Ramón. "Officer, take him away to the holding room."

Ramón nodded and left the room, pushing Hal in front of him.

Travis sat down and wondered. He was so close, but lacking testimony of Marco, there was still one piece missing. Who had recommended Gino to the Men's Dinner Club?

Chapter 40

The Jerry Connection

Ramón returned to the room where Travis was still pondering the coincidence of Hal running into Gino. It was a lucky break indeed for Vinnie, but it also meant that he had now run out of luck since he would end up in jail just like his father and his brother before. Although he believed that the woman had long broken with the mob and had written off her husband Rocky long before he died, Lucille might be upset. Her sons became operatives in the Fortimare family, and she never saw them again.

"Well, Hal's our first guy," Ramón smiled. "What about Vinnie Conti?"

"I'll get on the phone in a bit and get another warrant out. Any word on Marco?"

"Nothing so far. Can't we use the father as leverage?"

"Possibly, but that will require some cooperation by law enforcement in New York. Yesterday I met with the Chief of Police. I'll contact him first."

"Good. Also, I believe we haven't figured it all out yet, have we?" Ramón asked.

"Not quite indeed. We still don't know who introduced Gino to the Men's Dinner Club. Also, the fact that he agreed to join puzzles me because, as you have heard, he tried to lay low."

"Nevertheless, as Hal said, Gino became careless by moving here."

"I'd say so. Joining that quartet was a risky move, with both Phinn and Joe possibly figuring out who he was. He must have assumed that they didn't know him. Then there's Mike. I'm sure he never knew his name unless he'd taken a good look at the license posted on the taxi dashboard. Given the circumstances at the time, I doubt it. Plus, that's about two decades ago."

"So, we should talk to the club president again?"

"Perhaps. Marc already told us that the suggestion of the new member was anonymous. Then again, was it in written form, or a call?"

"We can always trace the call."

"Correct. Let's head out there. Give the man a heads up. I also want to talk to the ladies at the desk. Take along a copy of Hal's mugshot. Maybe there's more to find out."

"So, you think Mr. Whitman isn't involved anywhere in the story?"

"As far as I can tell, he's involved, perhaps unwittingly."

"It does take a special character to defend those thugs in the mafia, though. I'm not sure why I'm thinking this, but perhaps we haven't heard the last of Jim."

"I recall he said that he didn't suggest a new member for the group,"

"I know, but there has to be some significance for choosing that club. I mean, Gino could've joined a poker club and gone to the bathroom during that game. I think there is a reason. Besides that, I think it all went pretty quickly. He moves in, a few days later, he joins a club, and ten days later, he's murdered."

"All this has crossed my mind, Ramón. The whole set-up of coincidences is gnawing at me. We are missing something."

"Wasn't Jim Whitman one of the founders of that club?"

"He was. Where are you going with this?"

"Was this a way to keep an eye on a few people who had made life difficult for the mob, or, more specifically, for one of his clients? Perhaps even Mike Kreissman needed observation."

"You mean all of this is part of a larger plan, directed by a man lying in bed, recovering from a stroke?"

"What if the plan was different when it all started. The stroke complicated things and help was called in. Should we entertain this?"

Travis leaned back on his chair. He'd noticed that Ramón had been silent during most interactions with the people involved in this case. It looked like he listened and had come up with more questions for which Travis had no answer. These questions also sent the way of thinking about the case in a different direction. If the young officer was on to something, it was necessary to encourage him. Still, if that something led them in the wrong direction, the exercise would prove fruitless. In that case, perhaps the only lesson learned was that to evaluate all the options is good policing. "What you're saying, Ramón, is that we'll need to speak with Mr. Whitman again?"

"Not at this point in the investigation. I think Marc will do for now. The arrest warrants and the fact that one of Mr. Whitman's clients is in our custody may already shake the tree. Let's see what falls out. I assume we're not in a rush, are we?"

"Oh no, not at all. We have to get this right. Make that call, and we'll head over to the Arbors."

"Are we driving together?"

"Sure. We'll take my car. By the way, let's keep referring to Gino as Mr. Messina or Carlo."

Chapter 41

Curious George

Travis' phone rang the moment they got in the car. He looked at his screen. "Mr. Bender, what can I do for you?"

"I was wondering whether you can make it Thursday to our Murder Mystery Book Club?"

"I'm afraid I can't confirm at this point. We are still in our investigation, and..."

"Have you found the killer yet?" George interrupted.

"As I was about to say, we still have several loose ends to tie up. If I can wrap this up by tomorrow, I don't mind coming in and giving the members an update," Travis said.

"That would be great. I have one more question for you, detective. Did Carlo have any family?"

"We're following leads, Mr. Bender. All I can tell you is that if I do come on Thursday, I'll spring quite a surprise on your group regarding Mr. Messina.

"Oh, I can't wait," George said excitedly. "Let me know the status in the morning."

"I'll do that," Travis said and ended the call.

"Does he think that people in that club can help you with this case?"

"Not sure, he didn't suggest it as he's done before."

"Well, it's going to take a lot more detective work to nail all the parts by tomorrow."

"I agree," Travis said. "Let's go and see Mr. Baylor."

Chapter 42

Quartets And Answers

At Piedmont Hall, Melanie waived Travis and Ramón on as they walked in. They headed straight for the conference room. Marc Baylor hung up on a call as they entered.

"Detective, Officer, how can I help you?" Marc asked as all three sat down.

"We've made some headway in our investigation," Travis said, "But this has raised some more questions, and I believe you're the one to help us out with answers."

"I'll try," Marc said, all smiles. "What would you like to know?"

"How long has the men's club been around?"

"Jim came up with the idea about four years ago. We talked about it during a wine tasting evening, and within a week, he had the whole structure figured out."

"He didn't need any help with by-laws or anything?"

"Since he was a lawyer, he was the perfect guy. We never changed anything."

"And you became the first president?"

"That's the way Jim wanted it."

"I see, and how did the quartet set-up get started?"

"Again, that was Jim's idea. I kind of like it, you know. He often stressed that it would provide a strong relationship in a small cell as long as it was made up of four people who had a lot in common."

"And how were those first quartets put together?"

"Jim interviewed every member. Sometimes he or I would suggest someone for membership or a new member came with a name. Once we had sixteen members, we started making the foursomes. Jim did most of it, though."

"Did he put Mike, Phinn, and Joe together?"

"He did, he said they were all from New York or in law enforcement there, and since he was the lawyer, the quartet was established. I guess he'd done some casework in New York."

"Gotcha. So, that quartet has been together until Jim became ill."

"Correct. They seemed to get along very well together."

"I want to go back to what we discussed the evening of the murder. You mentioned that the nomination of the person to replace Jim came in anonymously. Did you have a feeling one way or another who might have done that?"

"None, detective."

"How exactly did this nomination reach you?" Ramón joined the conversation.

"I got a note in the club's box near the front desk."

"Handwritten or typed?" Travis asked.

"Handwritten. Neatly printed, I remember."

"Do you still have that piece of paper?" Ramón asked.

"We keep all notes in the box, so it's still in there. Why is that important."

"As you can imagine, we are trying to find out who nominated Mr. Messina."

"Would that be a big clue?"

"Yes, it would be. So, do you mind getting that paper for us? We need it for fingerprinting. Officer Acosta will bag it."

A few minutes later, Ramón put the small evidence bag on the table. "Ready for fingerprinting, detective."

Travis nodded. "Good, this may be a lucky break." He turned to Marc. "I do have a few more questions. Do you know who nominated Mike, Phinn, and Joe?"

"In the beginning and knowing we were shooting for sixteen members initially, the first four people became anchors, so to speak for a quartet. Jim was one of them. We then nominated people or picked them. We vetted each person, of course, and we didn't reject a single person."

"Is it fair to say then that Jim picked his quartet?"

"In effect, he did."

"Thanks. Officer Acosta, do you have any more questions?"

"I just have one," Ramón answered. "Do you know what kind of lawyer Mr. Whitman is?"

"I never asked him what kind of law he practiced," Marc admitted. "Is that important?"

"Perhaps," Ramón said. "He was a criminal defense lawyer."

Marc raised his eyebrows and thought about this revelation for a few moments. "I wonder what his connection was then to Phinn and Joe."

"Good point," Travis said. "Do you have any questions for us, Marc?"

"No, not really. I only hope that you guys solve this soon."

"Oh, I do think we're moving in the right direction," Travis said. "Thanks for your help, and if we can return that note to you, we'll let you know."

"Don't worry. No need," Marc said.

Chapter 43

ADA Parker's Take

It took less than an hour after retrieving the nomination notes for the results to come in. Travis looked over the technician's shoulder in the lab. Four clearly identified prints belonged to Hal Freese, the rest were those of Marc Baylor. Travis had Hal retrieved from the holding room in the building. He made a quick call and rattled off a few facts in the case regarding the man he would question momentarily.

Moments later, Ramón walked in with a now handcuffed man he guided to the chair at the table, opposite Travis. Ramón closed the door and remained standing. The detective opened the case file and pulled out a small plastic bag containing the note, holding it in front of Hal.

"Do you recognize this, Mr. Freese?"

Hal looked up and shook his head. "Nope."

"You wrote this about two weeks ago and dropped it off at the clubhouse. You said you went there a few times."

"Oh yeah? Maybe. Still, I'm not giving you anything more unless I get some relief from the DA's office. I've been here for two hours. What's going on?"

"I have some good news. The Assistant DA should be here momentarily."

"Good. I don't appreciate the handcuffs, by the way. Am I under arrest for something I didn't do?"

"Just a shortcut, Mr. Freese. It's easier when we charge you."

"Probably not going to happen when that ADA gets here. Why don't we just wait?" Hal asked.

"Fine," Travis said, put the bag back in the folder and walked outside while Ramón stayed in the room.

Assistant DA Parker arrived shortly after that. "What does he want?"

"The usual. Will give us more if we reduce the charges."

"Anything worthwhile?"

"As I told you earlier," Travis answered. "He may just point the finger at the man who set up the victim. We have a pretty good idea, but it needs to come from him. Once he pins that on the man we suspect, we can then link it back to Mr. Whitman. I'll fill you in after we finish with Mr. Freese."

"Let's go see him."

Hal couldn't wait to talk. Anything to get his out of jail card.

The ADA interrupted him. "Mr. Freese, slow down. I'll take all you say into consideration. However, at this moment, you will be charged as an accessory to murder. That will stay until we do a full evaluation of your case, and we'll discuss this with your attorney."

"I don't have one yet."

"Then I suggest you get one soon," the ADA responded. "Do you have someone in mind?"

"Yes, I do. Mr. Whitman."

Travis looked up. Mr. Whitman was in no shape to represent a client, and besides that, he wasn't even sure the man still had a license to practice. "May I suggest you ask him for a reference?"

"Oh, yeah. I'll do that. When do I get my call?"

"As soon as we finish here." Travis expected Hal to protest and request a lawyer by his side during this interrogation, but he didn't seem to mind. "You do have the right to counsel right now if you so desire," he said, adhering to policy.

"No, I'm okay," Hal said and continued. "I'm ready to tell you whatever you want to know."

"Noted," the ADA said. "Continue with your story."

Travis nodded in unison with Hal. "So, continuing where we left off, you dropped this note off at the clubhouse."

"I did. I did as I was told."

"Who told you to write the note?"

"Mr. Vinnie Conti."

"Okay, and this is after you reported Gino living at Carolina Arbors."

"Yes."

"Did Vinnie tell you where he got the idea of the club and the nomination?"

There was no hesitation this time. "My lawyer."

"You mean Mr. Whitman?"

"Yes. I don't see anything wrong with that."

"You want him as a lawyer, yet he set you up to drop off the note."

"I don't know anything about a setup. He must have had his reasons."

"I gather he did," Travis agreed. "What did you do after you delivered the note."

"Nothing. Mr. Conti was going to tell my lawyer that it was done, and the rest was up to Mr. Whitman."

"So, you were never in direct contact with Gino Barese?" Parker asked.

"No, sir. I didn't even contact Mr. Whitman."

"How about Mr. Conti?"

"He thanked me, and that's all that happened until I got that fake Uber call yesterday."

Travis nor Ramón reacted. The ADA replied. "Okay. I noted that. Let the detective know when you find a lawyer. I'll get in touch with him."

"You mean I can't go right now?"

"You may not. Officer," the ADA turned to Ramón, "I assume you read this man his rights. Return him to lockup."

Ramón walked out with a protesting Hal Freese, and ADA Parker sat down at the table.

"What do you think, detective?"

"Well, the scenario we envisioned is being confirmed one step at the time. We think Whitman started the club and came up with an ingenious idea to keep an eye on adversaries to the Fortimare family in the New York City area."

"Isn't one of those guys a cab driver? I mean, I understand the two police officers."

"We believe Mike Kreissman to have been the taxi driver who took Gino away from the towers."

"You told me about that a few days ago. Why would he need to be kept an eye on by Whitman?"

"I've been thinking about that, and I have come up with the only plausible answer. We know that Gino walked out of the towers and that people from the insurance office also got out. I bet you Vinnie saw him get into Mike's cab. While Mike didn't necessarily recognize our victim, it's unlikely that Gino remembered Mike from that short ride. However, I think Vinnie got that license plate and, with all his connections, traced that to Mike."

"Sounds reasonable," the ADA said. "How about Phinn and Joe?"

"Phinn's situation reminds me more of unfinished business. Beaten severely, he kept quiet, but who knows what would set him off to privately continue his pursuit to bring the Contis down. Joe was smart and could make a connection. Mr. Whitman wanted to keep an eye on them. What better way to do it via an invented Men's Dinner Club where everyone in a foursome had each other's back. The irony!"

"And then Gino shows up. Who was going to keep an eye on whom?"

"I suspect that once Gino, who remained a marked man, was no longer part of the quartet, a guy like Hal Freese could've moved to the neighborhood and taken his place. Mr. Whitman would've made that recommendation himself."

"The perfect guy to keep an eye on the other three."

"Right, but there's more. We figured that these three guys didn't end up at Carolina Arbors by accident. Again, we looked at Mr. Whitman, but we have no proof at this point."

Ramón walked in and heard the last part of the conversation. "Should we pick him up?"

"No need to do that just yet," Travis replied. "He's not going anywhere. Let's leave him under the impression that he cooperated with us and that we're all set."

"I see nothing wrong with that," the ADA said as Ramón nodded.

"All right. I'll try to get more confirmation on some of the things we believe happened and get back to you. Do you think you will need to cut a deal with Mr. Freese?"

"I'm not sure," the ADA said. "I'll discuss it with the DA."

Chapter 44

The Lure Of The Arbors

Travis updated Ramón on the conversation with Assistant District Attorney Parker. They had to make a decision. "Before we call Jim Whitman, let's check with the three members of the quartet. You call Mike, and I'll call Joe. We'll head over there, depending on what we hear. We need to talk to Phinn in person. We owe him, now that we have a better picture of what transpired years ago."

"Sounds like a plan," Ramón said and left the room. Travis returned to his office.

Travis made his call after checking on the status of the NY police bringing in Marco Conti. He saw no message or email or text message. A bit disappointed, he dialed. Joe answered.

"Malinski."

"Joe, this is detective Vinder."

"Right, how's the case going?"

"It's going well. I'm just filling some gaps, and I have just two questions for you."

"Go ahead."

"How did you decide to move to Carolina Arbors?"

"Wow. Let's see. We always knew we'd retire in the south. No question about that. We had our sight set on Florida, The Villages, to be honest."

"What changed your mind?"

"A flyer in the mail. I almost threw it out. The picture of the fountains at the entrance and the clubhouse piqued my interest. I started reading further and handed the flyer to my wife."

"Was the flyer addressed to you?"

"I don't recall. It may have been. All I know is that none of our neighbors got it. There was a number to call and claim a twenty thousand dollar discount. We discussed it, and we realized that the location was just about halfway between Orlando and New York. We already had friends in North Carolina. We checked with them on the weather there, and after a few days, we decided to call. Here we are."

"Did you get the twenty thousand off?"

"Sure did. The salesperson told us it came from a promoter. That did it for us."

"Okay. I don't assume you have the name of that promotor?"

"No idea. All we saw was that twenty grand was taken off the purchase price."

"I see. Thanks for the info, Joe," Travis said.

"Hold on. I have a question for you. Did the murder have anything to do with the mob in New York City?"

Travis was a bit surprised. "Yes, why do you ask?"

"I'm not surprised. Killing a guy from Jersey here usually originates from some sort of criminal element over there."

"I understand. Well, rest assured, Joe, we're onto the killer."

"Great. Well, if you need anything else, call me," Joe said and ended the call.

Travis dialed Phinn's number. He was playing Bocce Ball but could be home by eleven. He didn't seem surprised that Travis needed to talk with him.

Ramón walked into the office, smiling.

"Let me guess," Travis said. "Mike got a flyer in the mail for an incredible deal to move to Carolina Arbors."

"Joe told you the same thing, didn't he?"

"Yes, he did, and I expect to hear the same from Phinn. By the way, I'm heading over to his place. I want you to follow up on those arrest warrants. Vinnie Conti should've been picked up by now. Call me when you find out."

"Will do, Travis," Ramón said and headed back out.

Travis got to the O'Hara's house right at eleven o'clock. Mary met him at the front door and invited him in.

"Hi, detective," she said. Have a seat. Phinn's taking a quick shower. Would you like a cup of coffee?"

"Sure, thanks," Travis said.

From the kitchen, Mary asked: "Sugar, milk?"

"Just black is fine," Travis smiled as he sat down.

Mary put the cup on the side table.

"Mary, do you mind if I ask you a few questions?"

"Sure, what would you like to know?"

"You're aware that I've talked with your husband about the case. During my interview with him, Phinn mentioned that he went through some tough times after being roughed up by some criminals years ago."

"He didn't like to talk about that, you know."

"I fully understand that, however, he didn't seem to have a problem sharing it with me. Has anything changed recently?"

"I noticed that too. About three months ago, I heard him mention the episode to someone else. It was as if he'd finally come to terms with it. He started to share more with his friends."

"That's interesting. I need to ask Phinn about that."

"Amazingly, he's come a long way. He's more relaxed here, and even that has taken years."

"And how did you decide to move to this active adult community?"

"We've had North Carolina on our radar for quite a while. You see, about thirty years ago, our oldest son was at NC State on a soccer scholarship, and we made many trips down here. For a long time, we considered a move to Raleigh after Phinn retired. Then one day, we got a brochure in the mail about this area. The incentive discount offer that came with it made us decide. Then we found out we'd be in Durham, but oh well, it's still close to our grandchildren in Apex."

"So, a good decision then?"

"The best ever!" Mary said just as Phinn entered.

"What's the best ever?" he asked.

"Moving here, dear," Mary said as she got up. "You two talk. I'm going to take care of some things in the yard. More coffee is ready in the French press on the counter."

Phinn poured a bit of Jameson in his coffee and sat down. "So, how's the case going?"

"We had good progress. We identified the killer and the victim. I wanted to share that with you, but keep it to yourself for a while."

"That's good news. I gather you don't have the killer in custody yet, right?"

"True, but it's a matter of time."

"What do you mean by identifying the victim? We all know it was Carlo Messina."

"Not quite. Carlo was living under an assumed name. His real name, and hold on to your hat, was Gino Barese," Travis said and paused. He noticed Phinn's squinting eyes, tracking down the name in his past. It took less than ten seconds before Phinn lit up.

"Gino Barese? You're kidding. He was with that mob group that I followed. Wait a minute! Didn't he die during the attack on the Towers?"

"No, he didn't, but he used it as an opportunity to disappear for good by taking another person's identity."

"Holy crap! So, the Fortimare goons got to him after all..."

"Why would you say that?" Travis asked.

"He was wanted by the law as well as the mob. Now, I don't believe that New York's finest sent out a killer. But, how did they know Gino was still alive?"

"Do you remember an insurance company that acted as a front for the mob?"

"Insurance?" Phinn said and stared at the ceiling. "Yes, I vaguely do remember a questionable insurance outfit run by suspected mob people."

"Indeed. It's Bonelli and Partners. It's run pretty much by a fellow named Vinnie Conti," Travis said but was interrupted immediately.

"Rocky's kid! Son of a bitch! They must have figured that Gino hadn't perished at all on 9/11. That's wild," Phinn said as he got up to spike his coffee some more.

"It took us a while to piece it together, but the only real coincidence in this entire case is that Gino moved to this neighborhood and that an ex-mobster identified him."

"Do you mean there were possibly other coincidences?"

"For a while, we believed so, but that's for later. First, I have an important question for you."

"I'm getting curious now, especially wondering what this has to do with me."

"Okay. Tell me, did you ever mention your ordeal during your Men's Dinner Club meetings or with the people in your quartet?"

"The mafia came up in a conversation, I guess, several months ago. I think Joe mentioned something, and Jim laughed at it. That's when I told a bit of what happened to me, and that justice had never been served," Phinn said. "It came up a few more times because I was trying to remember names, but the subject was dropped soon after that."

"That sounds pretty much what I figured. Now, after Jim Whitman fell ill, how did you deal with that, given that your club touts the slogan *Having each other's back*? Did you look out for him, or did you right away look for another member?"

"Oh, no, not at all," Phinn exclaimed. "That wouldn't be right, you see. After his stroke and once he was home, we visited Jim, and he was supposed to recover. It wasn't until later that we realized he had too much trouble walking, and his speech was off. He himself suggested we should look for a replacement."

"Did you guys discuss a candidate?"

"We were in no rush, and about three weeks went by when we heard from Marc that we had a nomination."

"Anonymous, as far as you know."

"Correct. I feel you know more."

"Does the name Hal Freese ring a bell?" Travis asked, finishing his coffee.

"Hum," Phinn reflected. "Freese... The name sounds familiar, but I don't think I ever met a person named Hal... wait, wait! Freese, I recall someone with that name. Michael?"

"Close. It's Mikey."

Phinn shook his head. "Not sure, but there's something about that name."

"I know you have trouble remembering some things from the time of the assault on you, but we believe that it was Mikey Freese who was one of the thugs that beat you up."

"Really? Well, now I know. Is he still around?"

"We don't think so. Mikey spent some time in jail, thanks to Gino Barese. When Rocky got wind of what really happened in a murder case Gino was involved in, Gino became a target. Before anything happened, Rocky died, and his son Vinnie was tasked with the hunt for Gino."

"So a revenge killing after all."

"Indeed. Now, I need to come back to a few weeks ago and tell you about Jim Whitman as well as the killer and how it involves you."

Phinn sat up straight, puzzled, but listened patiently as Travis told him about the plot.

Chapter 45

Unraveling The Plot

Ramón got the news just before lunch. Both father and son Conti were in custody. They both lawyered up right away, but in Marco's case, the fingerprints, the pictures, and his collection of hunting knives with one missing, all sealed the case against him very quickly. With extradition hearings scheduled for next week, Marco would most likely be returned to North Carolina expediently. The young officer informed Travis, who was on his way back to the station. He also told him about Vinnie, who claimed total innocence. When presented with the phone call records between Hal Freese, Jim Whitman, and Marco, Vinnie had no wiggle room to avoid an arrest. It might be a bit of a challenge to prove that he ultimately gave the order to kill Phinn first and Gino later. All that, of course, had to be handled in North Carolina. In the case against Vinnie, the extradition battle would take longer as the lawyers had many shenanigans up their sleeve. Nevertheless, Travis was pleased with the progress. There was now only one more person to deal with: Jim Whitman.

Travis returned to the station and sat down with the DA, Assistant DA Parker, the captain, and Ramón. Pizzas were on the table as this was going to be a work lunch. Travis started by drawing a diagram on the whiteboard. He purposefully put Jim Whitman in a circle in the middle with lines running to the members of his quartet, to Hal Freese and to Vinnie Conti. Marco Conti's name was listed next to Gino Barese's name and had a link to both Jim Whitman and Vinnie.

"You believe that Mr. Whitman was the central figure then," the DA said.

"He controlled everything. Now, initially, his whole scheme with the men's club didn't include murder. It facilitated keeping an eye on people connected to old cases. No action warranted until, of course, they might become a threat to his client."

"That client being Vinnie Conti?" the ADA offered.

"I believe his main client was Ruggeri Bonelli. After the latter turned over the so-called insurance business to Vinnie, Conti became an implicit client," Ramón answered.

"What prompted sudden action in his clever scheme?"

"One of the members started talking about his days fighting the mob. Jim alerted Roger Bonelli, who then contacted Vinnie Conti. The latter one tasked his son with checking things out. Now, we have no proof yet of whether that assignment was the elimination of Phinn O'Hara. Still, his cover as a nurse for Mr. Whitman got him into the neighborhood."

The captain raised his hand. "So, we don't know for sure about O'Hara being Marco's target. That may give us some problems during the hearing, whenever that takes place."

"Not quite," Travis replied. "Given that nothing happened to Mr. O'Hara for weeks after Marco, aka Jerry Darcay, arrived here, may just be luck. I tend to believe that the opportunity had not arisen yet unless Mr. O'Hara talked more and more about his past and his quest against the Fortimare family," Travis explained. "However, what will stick in the arraignment is that we have Hal Freese's conversation with Vinnie about the bigger fish who exacted the toll of revenge. When Gino popped up, everything changed."

"And if they could kill only one person, it would have to be the traitor to the family," Ramón said.

"Indeed, Jerry left as soon as he killed Gino. In effect, Phinn was off the hook," Travis said.

"How does Mr. Whitman fit into the murder of Gino Barese, detective?" the DA asked.

"That is a matter of some facts and speculation," Travis admitted. "Mr. Whitman controlled events unfolding at Carolina Arbors. The fact that Marco Conti was sent down and had daily contact with the man must have resulted in Mr. Whitman finding out about Gino. We have no records of a conversation between the two, nor between Mr. Freese and Mr. Whitman. We're looking into their call records now."

"How incapacitated is Mr. Whitman?" the DA asked.

"Hard to tell. We've not contacted the man's physician, but we are about to do this."

"I gather that for now, and we can't take action. We can't charge the man for organizing a men's club, or hiring a male nurse, assassin or not. There's no crime in knowing that an ex-mob guy who killed both mafia and a law enforcement officer lived in the neighborhood," the DA concluded.

"I agree with you, sir," Travis said. "Until we get hold of phone records and messages, we have no proof, as for now, we can't confirm our suspicions."

"We'll make it our top priority to get a warrant for that information, rest assured," Parker added. "We'll convene again when we have the records and proceed with the correct charge."

Everyone agreed, and except for Travis and Ramón, everyone left the room.

"I wish we had hard evidence against Mr. Whitman," Ramón said. "As a lawyer, he was probably smart enough not to get caught. I bet you there are no written or verbal instructions except for messages to call him back, perhaps."

"Very true," Travis said, tapping his pen on the table. "He covered his butt, but he may have slipped up. Remember that his wife made a call, and perhaps she made more than one. Given his situation, she might have relayed messages."

"Wouldn't that be hearsay?" Ramón asked.

"Not if she's the one who heard the message directly, and she admits to it. Then again, she doesn't have to testify against her husband."

"I know," Ramón said, momentarily lost on thoughts. "Uh, I do seem to remember that Mr. Whitman had a notepad next to his bed. At the time, I didn't think anything of it, but perhaps there's incriminating information on it."

"This time, we would need a warrant. I don't believe our case is hard enough to get that from a judge. We need more than guesswork or assumptions."

"If Marco or Vinnie talked, wouldn't that help our case?"

"It would for sure. I'm not counting on it for now, though."

"So, where do we go from here?"

"I believe we need to bring in Mrs. Whitman. It may be too late to get her cooperation. Most likely, her husband has been alerted to the arrest of the Contis. In any case, I still want to talk to her. So have her picked up as soon as possible."

"Under suspicion of what?"

"Aiding and abetting the planning of a murder, giving refuge to a killer, posing as their private nurse, or whatever you can agree to with the ADA."

"No problem," Ramón said. I'll keep you posted.

Travis ended his call with Chief of Police Johnson in New York. They had twenty-four hours until they'd have to let Vinnie Conti go. Travis wasn't happy about that, and he knew that to make the arrest stick, it would depend on something incriminating that originated in Durham. He was pleased to see the text from Ramón pop up on his smartphone. Mrs. Whitman was on the way.

Mrs. Whitman didn't look any less annoyed than when they visited her the last time at her house. Travis welcomed her and had her sit down across from his desk. Ramón decided to pull up a chair on the side.

"Mrs. Whitman," Travis started. "You are well aware of our investigation, and we've already talked to you and your husband a few times. I didn't think it was feasible for him to join us today, so thanks for coming in."

"I had no choice, detective. Your officers forced me. They had a piece of paper. My husband is all alone. Thank God he's taking a nap. Now, what do you want this time?"

"You're not under arrest, Mrs. Whitman," Travis tried to reassure her. "We just have more questions, and I believe this time, you're the one who can help us out."

"Please keep it short. I need to get back to the house soon," she said, a little more relaxed.

"Sure. We'll keep it brief," Travis reassured her. "Now, did your husband ever refer to Jerry Darcay by a different name?"

"Not that I know."

"Okay. Did you talk to Mr. Conti in New York on more than one occasion?"

"The only person I called was Mr. Bonelli. I never called a man named Conti. Mr. Conti called us several times."

"And did your husband take those calls?"

"No, I usually pick up the house line or his cell phone."

"Good," Travis said. "Now, did you take any messages for Jim from Mr. Conti?"

"I usually handed the phone right over to Jim. Why?"

"Well, Jim may have been taking a nap like this afternoon, and I'm sure you didn't want to disturb him, right?"

"I guess that happened maybe twice."

"And how would you take the message? I mean, did you write something down or told Jim about it?"

"Oh, I'm quite forgetful. I always write things down."

"So, can you give me an example of what you wrote down?" Travis asked, hoping for a first glimpse of the conversation between the two men.

"Sure. I wrote down to call Mr. Conti back," Mrs. Whitman said.

Travis looked at Ramón. This interrogation was going a little less stellar than expected. He wasn't going to give up, though. "Perhaps at one point, you wrote a more extensive message down?"

Mrs. Whitman took a deep breath and stared away toward the mirror on the wall next to her. She shook her head and then shrugged her shoulders. "Perhaps one time, I guess," she said. "Mr. Conti told me to tell Jim that the old freezer case was important and that he should call Al."

Travis raised his eyebrows, but it was Ramón who spoke first. "Do you mean Hal, perhaps?"

"Al is what I heard."

"And freezer, perhaps it is Freese, a last name?"

"I don't know anyone by that name," she answered.

"Fine," Travis said. "Now, did you write down the number to call?"

"I did, and I'm sure my husband gave Al a call."

"Oh, good," Travis said and nodded toward Ramón.

Ramón left the room, and Travis continued. "Do you remember when you took that message?"

"Oh, I don't recall exactly, detective, but I'd say about two weeks ago."

"And do you still have that message?"

"I'm not sure. Why is that important? Jim isn't in any trouble, is he? I gave him the correct message."

"We're looking at some interactions right now, Mrs. Whitman," Travis said. "Another question: did you take any other messages from Mr. Conti?"

"There was one more a few days later, but that one I didn't write down because I was in the bedroom, and I told Jim right away. Jim had trouble speaking and didn't want to interact with anyone at that time."

"What did Mr. Conti tell you to tell your husband?"

"Just that a new member was going to join the club," she slowly said, making sure she remembered precisely.

"What did Jim say, after he heard that?"

"He just nodded."

"What do you think this message was all about?"

"Oh, Jim only belonged to one club, you know, that dinner club. I'm not sure how Conti knew about that if he was referring to the same club."

Travis didn't reply immediately. All this was too weak to finalize the case against Mr. Whitman. Having that note, though, would bolster it a bit. He would ask about it, but first, he needed to proceed with his line of questioning. "Did the name of that new member ever come up?"

"Not with me, detective. I do know Mike and Joe and the other fellow."

"Did the name Carlo come up?"

"You mean the man that was killed at the clubhouse?"

"Yes."

"Why would his name come up? You're not still suspecting we had anything to do with that, do you?"

"Just checking. One more thing, Mrs. Whitman. Do you possibly still have that note you wrote with Al's name on it?"

"I'll have to look for it. I clean up regularly, so I kinda doubt it."

"When the officers take you back home, why don't you look for it, and if you can find it, give it to them. Okay?"

"Fine, but I don't see how it can help you," she said. "Can I go now?"

"Sure, I'll ask the officers to take you home."

Both Travis and Mrs. Whitman stood up. She pushed the chair toward the desk, and as she turned to leave, she suddenly stopped. "You know, I don't recall that other fellow's name in the men's club, but I know that Jim often referred to Joe. He and the ex-detective got along well together."

"Oh, that's good to hear," Travis said, putting a folder under his arm.

"Yeah, a few times, he had a nickname for him. I can't recall what he called him last week when I overheard him talking to Mr. Conti. I'll ask him when I get home."

"Do that. Thanks for agreeing to come in," Travis said. He let her leave the room first after opening the door. The officers were waiting and escorted Mrs. Whitman out of the station to their car. Travis returned to his office.

Chapter 46

Motives

Travis stood by the front door. The search warrant covered more than combing through the Whitmans home — a broad sweep of warrants for phone records also provided a vehicle for the confiscation of those mobile phones. Mrs. Whitman had found that piece of paper earlier that afternoon and handed it to one of the officers who immediately bagged it. Although she was pleased to have been able to help, neither she nor her husband was happy having to unlock and turn over their cell phones. These also were bagged and taken to the station.

Having returned to the station, Travis stood in front of the whiteboard. ADA Parker and Ramón were sitting at his desk. "So, now we can confirm these links with just the messages alone. Mrs. Whitman only has a passive role in this case. But thanks to her note-taking, we do have confirmation of Mr. Whitman's active role through phone messages. He was careful, but not careful enough."

"So who ordered the murder of Gino?" the ADA asked.

"Oh, no doubt that was Vinnie Conti," Travis replied.

Ramón was curious: "What about Jim Whitman?"

"He coordinated and had Conti recommend Gino to the Men's Club. He also knew that Jerry was a cover name for Vinnie's son. From a message to Marco, we learned that as an ex-member of the club, he knew pretty much when the opportunity would be right."

"How would he know that Gino would walk into that bathroom at the right time last Saturday?" Ramón asked.

"Good question. Now, it's not surprising that people use the facilities, some more than others. Men tend to head there by themselves. It stands to reason that Gino would be alone in that locker room at one point in the evening. Marco probably hid in the showers. A simple peek around the corner would be enough to verify the person at the urinal."

"Why not kill him in his home or somewhere else?"

"All part of a plan to mislead us," Travis answered. "You see, having us spot a fuzzy look-alike of Mr. Whitman sent us to the one man in the neighborhood who was physically unable to commit the murder. Furthermore, the men's club activity provided a neutral setting, easy to get away from, and plenty of suspects."

"Are we ready to arrest Mr. Whitman?" Parker asked.

"The Captain is finalizing the warrant for his arrest and making medical arrangements, but yes, it will happen soon. All we need now is for the Contis to get here. Then it's all yours. I'll write my report, and then we're done with this case."

After the ADA left, Ramón wondered. "Well, this went quickly at the end."

"Just about. There are a few small items left, but why don't you join me tomorrow afternoon at the Arbors. I'm going to talk to the book club members. See if those sleuths can figure out some of what we found."

Chapter 47

Sleuths Meet With Vinder

There was a buzz in the conference room where the assembled sleuths discussed the little info they had on the case. George Bender was amazed at the number of comments, even though most were based on rumors. Everyone quieted down the moment Detective Vinder and Officer Acosta walked into the room. George introduced them, although most knew the detective and the officer from previous cases.

"Detective, thanks once more for spending some time with us," George started. He glanced around the table where most people nodded or verbally and softly agreed. "As you can imagine, many of us are curious when a police vehicle drives on our streets, or when a few of us spot you and the officer. Especially when you visit Piedmont Hall and various homes on our streets. One of my neighbors played pickleball the day after the murder and clearly heard the officer declare that he found the murder weapon; a hunting knife. So, we have caught bits and pieces, and besides some members of the Men's Dinner

Club which you visited, Jim Whitman seems to have been of particular interest."

"Goes to show, law enforcement officers don't operate in a vacuum," Travis said. A bit of laughter interrupted him. "So, clearly, this meeting is more of an update than a request for help in the case."

"What you're saying is that you've already solved the case?" Charlotte asked.

"Well, we have the killer in custody, we know the motive and have a solid grip on how it unfolded."

"Oh, we really don't have to help you this time?" Theresa asked.

"We can always use help. Perhaps we overlooked something, and that's when fresh eyes may bring something new to the case. I believe you all have read about so many criminal cases that you may have seen this one before. It's a bit like a writer devising a complicated plot, only to discover that someone has already written the story before."

Pete, one of the most avid readers in the group with at least fifty murder mysteries a year under his belt, was a bit anxious. "I beg to differ, detective. Motives tend to be similar, but the actual execution has distinctive and unique features. At least, that's my experience. If that weren't the case, I might stop reading."

"I guess that in this case, you will be pleased to hear the nuances, but of course, slicing someone's throat with a knife in a bathroom doesn't seem unique," Travis said.

"We can't wait to hear as much of the detail as possible," Theresa said. "Do you mind if we take notes?"

"Not at all," Travis said. He signaled Ramón to start the presentation.

Ramón unrolled a large sheet of paper with a diagram. It appeared similar to the one that was on the whiteboard at the office. Immediately, there was a buzz again when the sleuths noticed the name of Jim Whitman in the middle. Some knew Phinn, Mike, and Joe.

Travis raised his hand and had the full attention of the book club members. He told them about the plot, following a strict timeline, deviating a little at some points to give more background about Gino, Vinnie, and Rocky. When he revealed the identity switch prompted by the circumstances at 9/11, his listeners perked up - a bit of twist that they didn't see coming. As intriguing as it appeared, the story started to make sense. Judging by the comments, Travis gathered that the motive became a driving force that needed to culminate in the murder of Gino Barese, aka Carlo Messina.

Using the diagram taped to the wall, Travis pointed to the center figure: Jim Whitman. George was shaking his head. As a member of the club formed by the ex-member, he felt a bit uncomfortable. "So, without Hal Freese and his past, Gino might never have been recognized at the Arbors."

"Except for the fact that Joe did, at least at first," Charlotte said.

"I believe that the mob would've found him eventually," Arnold commented. "From what you told us, detective, they not only knew that Gino was still alive, but they never stopped looking for him. It was just a matter of time."

"I tend to agree," Travis said. "The fact that it happened here was circumstantial, but the club facilitated the plan."

"What if there hadn't been a club?" Pete asked.

"Good question," Travis answered. "Clearly, Mr. Whitman had full control of the men's club. It was a trap to keep an eye on people."

"So, more like *seeing* each other's back, than *keeping* each other's back," George said, sounding dejected. "Who knew?"

"While one can laud the idea of such a club, its premise wasn't so honorable," Travis said. "It was set up to attract possible troublemakers for the mob and gather them in one cell. Small fish in general until the big one came swimming in the pond."

"I wonder," Charlotte said. "Is it possible that he too received an offer he couldn't refuse?"

"I considered that briefly. Gino wouldn't have made it out of Jersey once located there. In summary, if he had stayed there, he might have lived," Travis answered.

"I have another question," Arnold said. "Have you figured out why Gino had to die at the first dinner?"

"Not really," Travis answered. "Once we get the Contis in our custody, we'll be pursuing that line of questioning. My gut feeling now is that Vinnie Conti wanted it done right away. Since his son had been in the neighborhood for so many weeks, he was suddenly useful before returning to New York City."

"But Whitman wasn't in any danger, right? I mean, he never met Gino, and the victim had nothing on him," Arnold persisted.

"That's true, but Jim Whitman set up Gino as a favor to Vinnie. They may have felt that their window of opportunity was closing."

"That ruse about looking like Mr. Whitman was clever," Theresa said. "I guess we need better video cameras on the premises."

There was a bit of laughter in the room. George took over. "Perhaps the dinner limited the number of people downstairs. That would prevent too many people from using the bathroom.

At that time at night, nobody would take a shower. So, I get it. But it also ruined our dinner."

"Mostly for the victim," Charlotte jumped in. "Detective, you mentioned something about Gino being careless in his crimes. His covert work among the small businesses was easily uncovered; his murder of Mikey's buddy, uh..."

"Tony, you mean," Travis clarified.

"Yes, Tony, that was sloppy, as you indicated. I wonder whether, as time went on, he became less and less aware of how he was letting his guard down. I'm surprised he didn't vet the club and the background of the other members in his quartet," Charlotte paused. "You can downright say that, after all his careful planning in taking another identity, in the end, he was sloppy again, and that led to his killing."

"Would it help you to know, Mrs. Beaumont, that he earned that nickname? It was referred to not only by Mr. O'Hara a few days ago, but it was also the one that Mr. Whitman used during his interrogation. You see, Mr. Whitman admitted that he'd made sure that someone invited *Sloppy Joe* for dinner."

THE END

Made in the USA
Columbia, SC
21 October 2020

23241162R00150